Madeleine L'Engle

WHO WROTE THAT?

LOUISA MAY ALCOTT
JANE AUSTEN
AVI
JUDY BLUME, SECOND EDITION
BETSY BYARS
BEVERLY CLEARY
ROBERT CORMIER
BRUCE COVILLE
ROALD DAHL
CHARLES DICKENS
THEODOR GEISEL
S.E. HINTON
WILL HOBBS
ANTHONY HOROWITZ
STEPHEN KING
MADELEINE L'ENGLE
GAIL CARSON LEVINE
C.S. LEWIS
LOIS LOWRY
ANN M. MARTIN
L.M. MONTGOMERY
PAT MORA
WALTER DEAN MYERS
SCOTT O'DELL
BARBARA PARK
GARY PAULSEN
RICHARD PECK
TAMORA PIERCE
EDGAR ALLAN POE
BEATRIX POTTER
PHILIP PULLMAN
MYTHMAKER: THE STORY OF J.K. ROWLING, SECOND EDITION
MAURICE SENDAK
SHEL SILVERSTEIN
JERRY SPINELLI
R.L. STINE
EDWARD L. STRATEMEYER
E.B. WHITE
LAURA INGALLS WILDER
LAURENCE YEP
JANE YOLEN

Madeleine L'Engle

Tracey Baptiste

Foreword by
Kyle Zimmer

Madeleine L'Engle

Chelsea House
An imprint of Infobase Publishing
132 West 31st Street
New York NY 10001

Library of Congress Cataloging-in-Publication Data
Baptiste, Tracey.
Madeleine L'Engle / Tracey Baptiste.
p. cm. — (Who wrote that?)
Includes bibliographical references and index.
ISBN 978-0-7910-9573-7 (hardcover)
1. L'Engle, Madeleine—Juvenile literature. 2. Authors, American—20th century—Biography—Juvenile literature. I. Title. II. Series.
PS3523.E55Z55 2009
813'.54—dc22
[B]
2008035033

Chelsea House books are available at special discounts when purchased in bulk quantities for business, associations, institutions, or sales promotions. Please call our Special Sales Department in New York at (212) 967-8800 or (800) 322-8755.

You can find Chelsea House on the World Wide Web at http://www.chelseahouse.com

Text design by Keith Trego
Cover design by Alicia Post

Printed in the United States of America

Bang EJB 10 9 8 7 6 5 4 3 2 1

This book is printed on acid-free paper.

Table of Contents

FOREWORD BY
KYLE ZIMMER
PRESIDENT, FIRST BOOK

HUMANITY IS POWERED by stories. From our earliest days as thinking beings, we employed every available tool to tell each other stories. We danced, drew pictures on the walls of our caves, spoke, and sang. All of this extraordinary effort was designed to entertain, recount the news of the day, explain natural occurrences—and then gradually to build religious and cultural traditions and establish the common bonds and continuity that eventually formed civilizations. Stories are the most powerful force in the universe; they are the primary element that has distinguished our evolutionary path.

Our love of the story has not diminished with time. Enormous segments of societies are devoted to the art of storytelling. Book sales in the United States alone topped $24 billion in 2006; movie studios spend fortunes to create and promote stories; and the news industry is more pervasive in its presence than ever before.

There is no mystery to our fascination. Great stories are magic. They can introduce us to new cultures, or remind us of the nobility and failures of our own, inspire us to greatness or scare us to death; but above all, stories provide human insight on a level that is unavailable through any other source. In fact, stories connect each of us to the rest of humanity not just in our own time, but also throughout history.

This special magic of books is the greatest treasure that we can hand down from generation to generation. In fact, that spark in a child that comes from books became the motivation for the creation of my organization, First Book, a national literacy program with a simple mission: to provide new books to the most disadvantaged children. At present, First Book has been at work in hundreds of communities for over a decade. Every year children in need receive millions of books through our organization and millions more are provided through dedicated literacy institutions across the United States and around the world. In addition, groups of people dedicate themselves tirelessly to working with children to share reading and stories in every imaginable setting from schools to the streets. Of course, this Herculean effort serves many important goals. Literacy translates to productivity and employability in life and many other valid and even essential elements. But at the heart of this movement are people who love stories, love to read, and want desperately to ensure that no one misses the wonderful possibilities that reading provides.

When thinking about the importance of books, there is an overwhelming urge to cite the literary devotion of great minds. Some have written of the magnitude of the importance of literature. Amy Lowell, an American poet, captured the concept when she said, "Books are more than books. They are the life, the very heart and core of ages past, the reason why men lived and worked and died, the essence and quintessence of their lives." Others have spoken of their personal obsession with books, as in Thomas Jefferson's simple statement: "I live for books." But more compelling, perhaps, is the almost instinctive excitement in children for books and stories.

Throughout my years at First Book, I have heard truly extraordinary stories about the power of books in the lives of children. In one case, a homeless child, who had been bounced from one location to another, later resurfaced—and the only possession that he had fought to keep was the book he was given as part of a First Book distribution months earlier. More recently, I met a child who, upon receiving the book he wanted, flashed a big smile and said, "This is my big chance!" These snapshots reveal the true power of books and stories to give hope and change lives.

As these children grow up and continue to develop their love of reading, they will owe a profound debt to those volunteers who reached out to them—a debt that they may repay by reaching out to spark the next generation of readers. But there is a greater debt owed by all of us—a debt to the storytellers, the authors, who have bound us together, inspired our leaders, fueled our civilizations, and helped us put our children to sleep with their heads full of images and ideas.

WHO WROTE THAT? is a series of books dedicated to introducing us to a few of these incredible individuals. While we have almost always honored stories, we have not uniformly honored storytellers. In fact, some of the most important authors have toiled in complete obscurity throughout their lives or have been openly persecuted for the uncomfortable truths that they have laid before us. When confronted with the magnitude of their written work or perhaps the daily grind of our own, we can forget that writers are people. They struggle through the same daily indignities and dental appointments, and they experience the intense joy and bottomless despair that many of us do. Yet somehow they rise above it all to deliver a powerful thread that connects us all. It is a rare honor to have the opportunity that these books provide to share the lives of these extraordinary people. Enjoy.

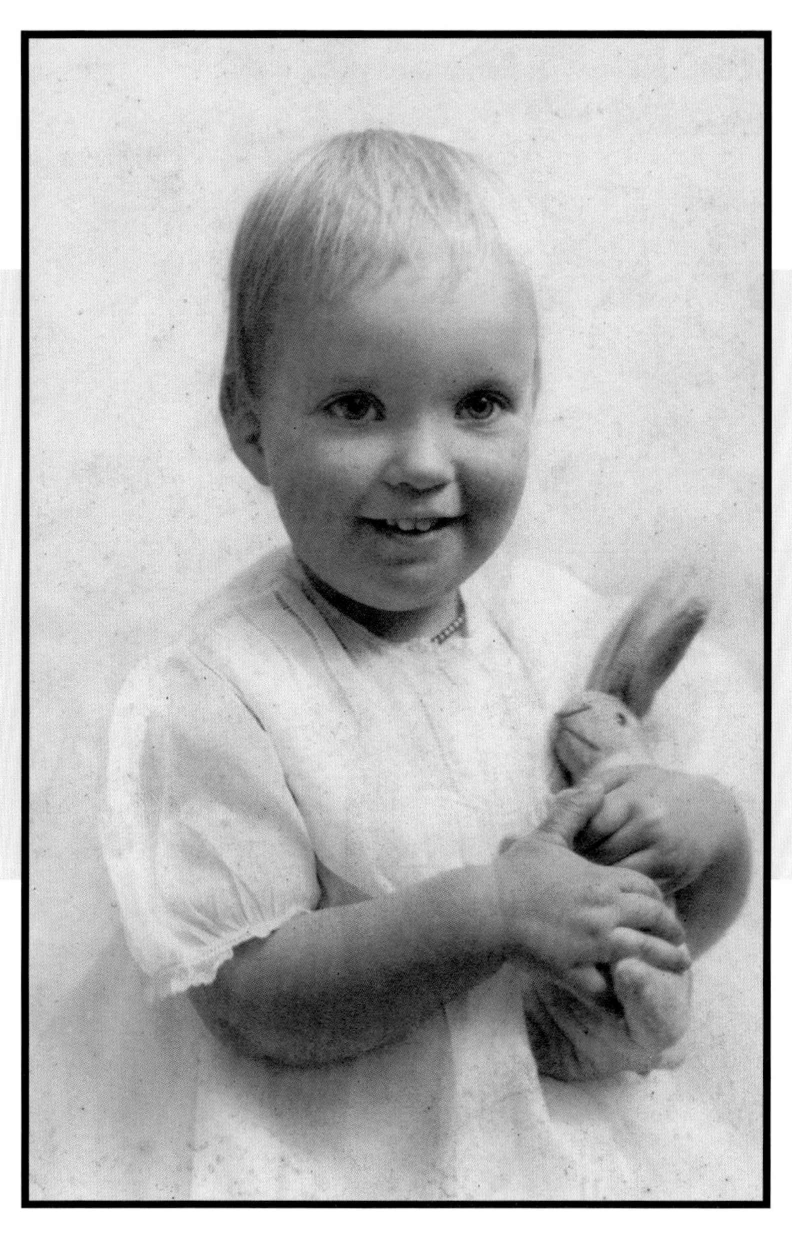

A photo of Madeleine L'Engle Camp as a child. L'Engle did not have a close relationship with her parents, who were middle-aged when she was born. Set in their ways and used to a lifestyle not suitable for young children, her parents left L'Engle to be raised by her nanny, Mrs. O'Connell.

1

A Born Writer

MEET THE CAMPS

Madeleine L'Engle Camp was born on a cold, snowy Thanksgiving night in New York City to Madeleine Barnett and Charles Wadsworth Camp. Her father was overseas at the time, fighting in World War I. It was November 29, 1918. Madeleine's mother was not well, and her doctor feared that she would not be able to carry the baby to term. To stay healthy, she spent most of the nine months of pregnancy in bed. Madeleine's grandmother came up from Florida to help. On that snowy night when Madeleine's mother finally went into labor, the soon-to-be grandmother, stepped out into the blizzard-like weather to find a taxi.

The wind made a mess of the older woman's hair. There were no taxis to be found. Fortunately, a couple of strangers stopped to help. They took Madeleine's mother and grandmother to the hospital, where Madeleine was born. She was named after her great-grandmother, Madeleine L'Engle. Charles Camp couldn't get leave to come home, so he did not see his first and only child for several months.

Even before she was born, Madeleine's family history made for interesting storytelling. Her maternal grandfather nearly lost a leg at the age of nine when he accidentally stabbed himself while using a knife to whittle wood. He hit an artery, and the wound would not stop bleeding. The one doctor in town knew only to bandage it with a piece of wood to try to stop the bleeding. For two weeks, he remained bandaged like that until his leg was swollen and black. When a Civil War surgeon came through town, he said that the leg would have to be amputated—or cut off—because the surgery was too risky. They did take the risk, though, and performed the surgery on the kitchen table. It was a success, and her grandfather went on to become a brilliant athlete. He was named Bion Barnett. Barnett married Caroline Hallows L'Engle, and L'Engle's mother, Madeleine, was their daughter. Her father was the chairman of the board of Barnett Bank in Jacksonville, Florida; he was both wealthy and well known. One day, he left his wife suddenly and moved to the south of France, leaving only a note on the mantel in their home. "The Barnett scandal was just incredible for Jacksonville,"[1] Madeleine's cousin said.

Madeleine's parents had had a long life together before she was born. Camp was a foreign correspondent for a newspaper before he joined the army. He was often sent on assignments all over the world, sometimes taking his wife on these adventures with him. Years later, L'Engle would write: "[My mother's] pre-motherhood existence was exotic and adventurous; in the days before planes, she traveled by camel and donkey."[2] Her father's time as a correspondent ended when he enlisted in the armed forces.

During World War I, L'Engle's father had been injured by mustard gas. The gas affected his lungs badly. At least, this is what L'Engle claimed. Her cousin, Francis Mason, however, had never heard anything about his uncle having bad lungs. He told Cynthia Zarin, "Uncle Charles was not ailing in his life. He was a big, handsome man in a white linen suit smoking cigarettes on the porch and drinking whiskey. He was a favorite of my mother's, and she was a talker, and she never mentioned anything about him being gassed in the war."[3] When he returned from fighting in the war, ill from the gas, he stopped working as a correspondent. Instead, he decided to become a writer. He wrote stories, movies, and plays. He worked in an office in the famous Flatiron Building in New York City.

Madeleine's parents loved art and culture. They lived in New York City and made friends with many artists, actors, and singers. Her father belonged to the Opera Club and enjoyed attending matinee performances. Mrs. Camp was an accomplished pianist who had studied music in Berlin, Germany. She liked to have singers from the Metropolitan Opera come to the house. They would all gather around the piano, where she played for them and they sang. Young Madeleine grew up with different kinds of artists regularly visiting her parents' house for Sunday dinners.

By the time that Madeleine was born, her parents were already an older couple. They had been married nearly 20 years. Her mother was almost 40 years old. They were set in their ways, and their lifestyle did not suit children. They kept late hours and went out often. They also had very different ideas on how to raise their daughter. Madeleine's mother wanted her to be graceful and confident. She believed that if she was raised by a dancer or a circus performer, she would learn these traits. Madeleine's father was horrified by the thought; he believed that children should be raised by a nanny and have dinner on a tray in the nursery. He wanted a traditional English upbringing for his daughter, and that is exactly what she got. A nanny named Mrs. O'Connell was hired to raise young Madeleine.

Madeleine called her nanny Mrs. O. She was a very kind woman. Although she was hired to bring Madeleine up in a strict environment, she made sure that there was enjoyment, too. For example, she sometimes bought Madeleine sweets or mixed her oatmeal with sugar. Mrs. Camp did not want Madeleine to have sugar in her oatmeal, so she always tasted it to be sure. Mrs. O put the sugar on the bottom of

Did you know...

L'Engle's father encouraged her writing. When she was 10 years old, he gave her an old manual typewriter that he had used when he was a foreign correspondent before World War I. L'Engle continued to use it as an adult, but it was problematic: She had to write all her drafts longhand because the *e* always slipped on the typewriter. To type, she needed to use a pair of pliers and a hammer. After she had written about eight books, her agent begged L'Engle's husband to buy her a typewriter that actually worked.

the bowl, though, and stirred it in after her mother tasted it. Her mother never understood why Madeleine would only eat oatmeal for Mrs. O.

Madeleine did not see much of her parents when she was young. They went out often and had parties at the house, which their daughter was not allowed to attend. Sometimes Madeleine would sneak in and listen to the party music from behind the couch. The guests at the parties may have seen her hiding there, but they never told her parents—and her parents never found her out.

Madeleine's mother and Mrs. O read stories to her every day. She usually ate alone in her nursery, with her feet up on her desk and a book in one hand. The only meal she had with her parents was on Sundays at noon. During these meals, the family was so unfamiliar with each other that her parents barely had anything to say to her. Because she lived somewhat apart from her parents, Madeleine turned to her library full of books for entertainment. Once she had read and re-read her books, she decided to write a few of her own.

L'Engle later recalled, "I wrote my first story when I was 5. It was about a little G-R-U-L, because that's how I spelled 'girl' when I was 5."[4] Her mother kept that story for a long time. In fifth grade, she attempted to write her first novel. Her early interest in writing was fortunate, as her writing helped her to cope with difficult experiences at school. Madeleine enjoyed her brief time at Oberlin, a small private school for students in grades one through three. There, she learned to read and write well. After Oberlin, Madeleine attended another private school. Sadly, her experience at this new school was not positive. The teachers did not believe she could write. As a matter of fact, according to L'Engle, they believed she was stupid.

It is no surprise that she hated that school, and so much so that throughout her life she refused to say which school she had attended.

SCHOOL DAYS

At this second school, athletics were important. Unfortunately, Madeleine had a few physical problems. An illness early in her life had made one leg shorter than the other, and she had to wear a brace on one foot. When she was tired, she walked with a limp. It made her very clumsy at sports. She was always chosen last for teams during sporting events. The other students would groan with dismay when she was chosen to be on their team—they knew they would lose. She was quite unpopular, and sometimes she was even bullied. Madeleine felt very solitary as an only child and without any friends at school. She tried without success to shrug off her classmates' unkindness. It was a sad time for her, but Madeleine did not go to her parents to complain. She knew that she would have to go to school anyway, so she endured it silently.

It is unclear what made her teachers think she was not a good student. However, L'Engle later wrote that her teachers were actually the ones responsible for making her a writer. Because they assumed she was stupid, she did not pay much attention to her schoolwork. She later recalled:

> I learned that there was no point doing homework. It was going to be pushed down. And so instead of doing homework, I would dunk my books and think of myself as the non-achiever, and then I would move into the real world where I wrote stories. And I wrote because it was my survival system.[5]

Madeleine also read as much as she could when she was a child. Her favorite was *Emily of New Moon* by Lucy

Maud Montgomery, who also wrote *Anne of Green Gables.* Madeleine and the character Emily had a lot in common: Emily wanted to be a writer, she had a father who had lung problems, and she knew there was more to the world than facts. Like Emily, Madeleine began to keep a journal. This habit of journal writing continued as an adult. In *A Circle of Quiet*, L'Engle said that it is essential for a writer to keep a journal and write in it every day.

When she was a young girl, keeping a journal was not a popular thing to do. She was not asked or encouraged to write by anyone in her family or her teachers. She began when somebody gave her a notebook that she thought was very pretty. "I used to love to go into stationery stores and look at the pretty notebooks, particularly when I was in France and saw the notebooks with the marbleized covers and the little leather corners," she said. "You couldn't see a notebook like that and not want to write in it."[6] Madeleine also read fairy tales, myths, science fiction, and fantasies. She particularly liked the authors E. Nesbitt, Jules Verne, and H.G. Wells.

When Madeleine was in sixth grade, the school held a poetry competition. She decided to enter. She said that it was lucky that her homeroom teacher did not have to review her work before she sent it in. If she had, L'Engle thought it never would have been included in the competition. She wrote the poem, submitted it, and it won. Her teacher did not believe it. "Madeleine couldn't possibly have written that poem. She must have copied it from somewhere. She's not very bright, you know,"[7] her teacher said, according to Donald R. Gallo. Madeleine's mother went into her school and brought with her all the stories that Madeleine had written when she should have been doing her homework. The teacher then realized that Madeleine had in fact written the poem.

Pictured above, Margaret Clapp in traditional cap and gown as president of Wellesley College in Massachusetts. Earlier in her life, Clapp had been one of the few teachers in L'Engle's life who encouraged her writing and advised her to read challenging books.

Even though Madeleine was clearly miserable, and the school was not the right place for her, her father decided that she should stay for the rest of the school year. He had not wanted her to attend that school in the first place, and he thought that leaving her there would teach her mother a lesson. The following September, thankfully, she was allowed to transfer to a different school.

Madeleine spent the next year at the Todhunter School, another private school in New York City. She was taught by Margaret Clapp, who was a new teacher at the time. Clapp recognized Madeleine's writing talent immediately and encouraged her to write and to read difficult books. Clapp's attention boosted Madeleine's confidence. She began to work harder at school. More important, she was happy. Clapp, a fine and gifted teacher, went on to become the first woman president of Wellesley College. Unfortunately, Madeleine's time at Todhunter soon came to an end. Because of his weak lungs, her father became ill with pneumonia, a disease that affects those organs. He spent many weeks in the hospital. This was an ongoing problem that began with his experience in the war.

The Camps were advised to move away from New York City. Mr. Camp's doctor felt that the city air was too dirty for him and that another bout of pneumonia could be fatal. The family decided to move to Europe, where the air was better and her father could breathe more easily. They moved in 1929, when Madeleine was 12 years old.

THE ALPS

The Camps moved to a chateau, or house, near the town of Chamonix in Switzerland, near the French Alps. The chateau had no running water. Water was brought in every day in big china pitchers that sat inside of matching washbowls. Madeleine spent the summer roaming through the old house. Her father, however, was not the only one who was sick. Her mother, considered "frail," became ill easily. Often, Madeleine's mother would have to spend time in bed and a housekeeper would run the house. When the family moved to Europe, the conditions were hard for her mother, but her father was the main concern. One day, Madeleine walked into her parents' room and saw her mother lying in bed, her face showing all the misery she felt about living in Europe. Madeleine left the room quickly and quietly before her mother knew she was there.

At the end of the summer, her parents drove her to an English boarding school, where she was introduced to the headmistress. As Madeleine was shaking hands with the headmistress, she said that her parents simply disappeared. She had no warning that she would be left there, and she felt abandoned. At this school, students were assigned a number, and that is what they were called. She was number 97. L'Engle said that even when her schoolmates used her name, they mispronounced it. Madeleine disliked the conformity of being called by number instead of name. She believed that taking away a person's name was to take away his or her reality. That brush with conformity left a bad impression on Madeleine. In her most famous work, *A Wrinkle in Time,* the source of all evil tries to inflict conformity on the universe.

While at the boarding school, Madeleine had a few more run-ins with teachers. One day, she had gotten into trouble and was being reprimanded in front of everyone. She began to play with her dental work. It was a plate with false teeth that she wore because some of her teeth had not grown in. The teacher thought she was chewing gum, held out her hand, and told her to spit out what was in her mouth.

A photo of a village in the French Alps. L'Engle moved with her parents to the Alps from New York City in order to improve her father's health, which had been damaged after he had been gassed in World War I.

Madeleine spat out her dentures. The other students were thrilled! There is no record of whether she was punished for this act of defiance or not.

In *Walking on Water,* L'Engle talked about how artists improve because they have suffered. Just like Ludwig van Beethoven, a composer who was deaf, and John Milton, the blind author of *Paradise Lost*, she saw that some artists used art, such as music, painting, or writing to work through their struggles. Like these artists, L'Engle suffered as a child because she had physical problems and because she had been treated so badly by some teachers. The adversity, she believed, made her a better writer. "We do learn through pain,"[8] she said. There was more pain to come.

BACK IN THE STATES

The Camps remained in Europe for a number of years and only returned to the United States when Madeleine's grandmother became seriously ill. The family found a beach house in Florida near her grandmother. They named it Illyria. Though her grandmother's health improved, her father's condition remained poor. Madeleine enjoyed swimming in the ocean and sitting on the beach to daydream. Sometimes, when her father was well enough, they went for walks along the beach together. On these walks, she recited her poems to him. He nodded politely when he heard them. If he commented on a poem, Madeleine knew that he really liked it and that it was good.

At the end of the summer, Madeleine was sent to Ashley Hall, a prestigious school in Charleston, South Carolina. The school's mission is to provide "a challenging and rewarding academic environment for girls and young women."[9] Former First Lady Barbara Bush also attended Ashley Hall. Of her time at the school, L'Engle said, "I don't want to lose any part of who I was at Ashley Hall. It is an essential part of who I am now. I don't ever want to forget sitting high up in the limbs of a live oak tree and reading [Leo] Tolstoy's *Anna Karenina*."[10]

At Ashley Hall, Madeleine finally had teachers once again who saw her potential. She was 14 years old when she began to attend classes there, and Madeleine was happy at school for the first time in her young life. She felt appreciated as a leader. Her only problem occurred at school dances because she was so tall. She stood almost head and shoulders above any boy with whom she might have danced. Fortunately, the school dances were only held once or twice a year.

Unfortunately, the dances at Ashley Hall were not the only dances Madeleine had to endure. Because her mother was from a wealthy southern family, she was often invited to debutante balls. Debutantes are girls from important families who have "coming-out" parties to introduce them to society. Madeleine, still clumsy and tall, was not good at small talk. In addition, because she did not grow up in Florida, she also did not know the girls at the debutante balls. She did not know the boys who were their dates, either.

No boy ever called her for a date; all her dates were arranged for her. To make matters worse, seafood was often served at these parties. Madeleine was allergic to seafood, but at the time she did not know. During dinner, she would get sick and have to leave often to throw up in the bathroom. At times, Madeleine created a distraction for herself to escape from the party. For example, she would rip the hem of her dress so that she could hide in the bathroom for a while. Madeleine was very unhappy at these parties, and her odd behavior made her quite unpopular.

Two years after the family moved to Florida, Madeleine received a letter at school from her mother. Her father was ill again. He had gone up to Princeton University to see a football game at his old college. While there, he came down with pneumonia again. When he returned to Florida, he had to be hospitalized. Her mother asked Madeleine to pray for him. Madeleine mailed some of her poems to him that she thought her father would like. Unfortunately, they would not arrive in time. The next morning, the school principal, Mary Vardine McBee, told Madeleine to take the evening train back to her home in Florida. By the time she got home, her father had died. She could not bring herself to cry or show any outward emotion. She wondered what had happened to her father. She wondered where he was, or if he had simply stopped existing. Before her father died, Madeleine's stories mostly involved the world of fairy tales. Afterward, she wrote stories that were based firmly in reality. The fairy tales were over.

After her father's funeral, Madeleine returned to Ashley Hall to complete her last year of school. She was very active that year. The previous year, she had been a member of the student council. In her final year, she was voted the student council president. Madeleine did not know what she should do when she graduated in May. Her principal, McBee, advised her to try Smith College. It was a highly selective all-girl school. On their Web site, the school describes itself as the "largest liberal-arts college for women"[11] in the United States. College would be expensive, but Madeleine could afford to go there because her grandfather had set up a trust fund for all his grandchildren's education. To get into the school, Madeleine would need to pass college entrance tests. She did not think that she could do it, but McBee encouraged her to try. She enrolled in classes to prepare her for the tests in the summer. After she took the tests, she and her mother left for a vacation in Europe. She decided that if she did not get into Smith, she would remain in Europe and write a novel. In the end, her math scores were low, but her long answers to the English questions impressed the professors at Smith College, and she was accepted. Madeleine was still in Europe when she received her acceptance letter. She left quickly for Florida, and then packed her bags for college.

The dormitory entrance of Smith College in Northampton, Massachusetts. L'Engle's time at the liberal arts college proved to be enormously beneficial for her development as a writer.

2

The Actress

HER OWN LIFE

Smith College in Massachusetts was another happy school experience for L'Engle. It was during her time there that she really learned how to be a writer. Her creative writing courses, among other things, taught her that she needed to start her story where she thought it should start; then, later on, she learned to cut at least the first paragraph. She believed that writers need to write out their beginning of the story and through that find where the story actually begins.

Because the school did not have a literary magazine, L'Engle and a friend decided to create one. L'Engle wrote poems, short stories, and plays while at Smith. Much of her early work was published in the literary magazine that she had started. Some of her plays were also produced by Smith students for the public. One year, a poem she had written won the college's Elizabeth Babcock Poetry Prize. This time, there was no question that L'Engle was the author. Her peers and professors knew that she was very talented. In addition to the honor, the award also came with a $2,500 prize—a considerable amount of money at the time.

In college, L'Engle sometimes skipped classes that she considered a waste of her time—usually, anything that was not a writing or English class. This did not mean that L'Engle was idle. She learned to work hard in college, and her grades were always high.

While at Smith, she met and studied with Mary Ellen Chase, who later became a novelist. Chase divided English literature into three sections: major, minor, and mediocre. L'Engle and her other friends who wanted to be writers had immediate reactions. "We were all quite vocal about not wanting to be mediocre!" she said. For L'Engle, her only option was to become a famous writer. There was nothing else. "It didn't occur to me that there was an alternative career,"[1] she said.

On breaks, she went home to Florida, where debutante balls and arranged dates waited for her. By then, her mother was living in an apartment in Jacksonville, Florida. Financial troubles had forced her to sell the beach house, Illyria, not long after L'Engle's father died. Occasionally, on weekends during the school year, L'Engle visited some of her cousins in Pennsylvania. One of the cousins, Starr, was a book reviewer and often provided L'Engle with new books to read.

After graduating from Smith, L'Engle did not return to Jacksonville. She moved to New York City and found an apartment with her college roommate in Greenwich Village on West Ninth Street. To cut costs, they also shared it with a few other aspiring artists. L'Engle used the old furniture and china that her parents had in storage to furnish the small apartment. While in New York, she dreamed of being published. She sent out stories to small magazines and university papers. It was at this time that she decided to drop her last name and go by her first and middle names, Madeleine L'Engle. At first, her mother was upset about the decision to stop using her father's name. She thought that this was rejecting her father. L'Engle assured her that she was not. Because her father had been a writer for a number of years, many people at publishing houses knew who he was. L'Engle did not want to have her work chosen because she was Charles Camp's daughter. She wanted to be a writer on her own merit. Eventually, L'Engle's mother understood her decision.

While many magazines published L'Engle's stories, those publications did not pay much. She needed a real job. Throughout high school and college, she had done

Did you know...

The Harold D. Vursell Memorial Award grants $10,000 each year to a writer whose work merits recognition for the quality of its prose style. The award was established by the American Academy of Arts and Letters and was first awarded in 1982.

some acting. In high school, she had often played male roles because she was so tall. In college, she had the opportunity to play female roles too. L'Engle did not feel that she was really trained to be an actor, but theater hours were exactly what she needed to give her time to write, and the pay was $65 per week. She also found work through the American Theatre Wing selling war bonds. She would go from theater to theater on Broadway with the bonds. During intermission, she would sell as many as she could, then she could sit in any empty seat and watch the show. L'Engle saw many Broadway shows this way and used the experience as her acting training. After a few months, she felt ready to audition for a play. A few days after the audition, she received a call saying that she had gotten the job. It was as an understudy, but it was still paying work.

She moved a couple of times and finally found an apartment of her own at 32 West Tenth Street. The composer Leonard Bernstein lived upstairs. He and his wife had two young children, and he and L'Engle talked about switching apartments so that they would not have to carry the baby carriage up the steps.

L'Engle took acting lessons from the famous actor Morris Carnovsky for the small sum of a quarter per lesson. She was finally leading her own life. She made sure that she was not in Jacksonville during debutante season, so she could avoid being forced to attend balls.

Eventually, the play, *Uncle Harry,* went on tour. L'Engle went along. She worked on her novel backstage every chance she could. As soon as it was ready, she sent it to Vanguard. She had chosen Vanguard because the publisher, Jim Henle, had seen her work in some literary magazines. He asked if she was working on a novel, so she sent it to

Madeleine L'Engle, probably in her early twenties. At this time in her life, L'Engle was working—quite successfully—as both a writer and as a stage actress.

him. The publisher decided to buy it. Her advance was $100, and L'Engle was assigned Bernard Perry as an editor. His notes directed her how to fix what L'Engle later called "the shapeless mass of material"[2] that was her manuscript. She had until the end of the summer to work on it. The play ended in the spring, leaving her the entire summer free to perfect her writing. Unfortunately, even at that time, it was impossible to live for an entire summer on $100, and so she returned to work selling war bonds.

When Vanguard finally published her first book, *The Small Rain,* it sold very well. She arranged to have her royalties, the money that she made from the book, paid to her monthly so that she could have a salary for a few years. It worked out that her monthly check from Vanguard was $250—more than enough for her to live on at the time.

This first novel echoed L'Engle's life in many ways. It began with 10-year-old Katherine Forrester, who was being reunited with her mother after three years. Her mother was a pianist, like L'Engle's mother, and an accident had ended her musical career. Soon after they were reunited, Katherine's mother died. She was then sent to a boarding school in Switzerland, where she began to develop her own gift for playing piano. The story concluded with Katherine, a talented young woman, being faced with a choice between her art and the man she loves. L'Engle continued Katherine's story in *A Severed Wasp,* which was published in 1982—nearly 40 years after the original novel. In that story, Katherine was in her seventies, and she was retiring from a long and successful musical career.

With the publication of her novel, L'Engle was earning a salary in the theater and was also a paid writer. L'Engle did not seem to celebrate her accomplishment of becoming a published writer. Perhaps because she felt so sure that she would do it, being published was no big deal.

MRS. FRANKLIN

After *Uncle Harry* closed, L'Engle was cast in *The Cherry Orchard.* When she went to her first rehearsal, she met Hugh Franklin, the actor cast to play the lead. She recalled, "I saw a very tall, thin young man with black hair and enormous, very blue eyes. I had never seen such eyes."[3] He invited her out to lunch and the two talked until two in the morning. They had spent nearly 10 hours together. When L'Engle returned home to her apartment, she thought, "I have met the man I want to marry."[4]

Franklin and L'Engle became a couple very quickly during *The Cherry Orchard*'s run. It seemed as though they were being pushed together by the rest of the cast. Franklin, however, was not the only love that L'Engle found through that play. The play had a part for a dog. Cast members who owned a dog felt that his or her pet should have the part, but none of their animals were calm enough for the role. Eventually a small poodle was bought specifically for the play. After just a few days, it became clear to everyone that the dog liked L'Engle best. She took care of him during rehearsals and backstage during the show. They named him Touché (too-SHAY)—a word used to acknowledge the appropriateness of a point.

The play went on the road in the winter, and L'Engle had a difficult time finding a hotel that would take her dog. One night, they tried every hotel in Baltimore and did not find a place until about one in the morning. The hotel was old, cheap, and dirty, but she had no choice. Despite the difficulties she found on the road, L'Engle's relationship with Franklin was going well, so nothing mattered. That is, until one day he suddenly and without explanation stopped spending time with her. L'Engle never asked what had happened, but by the time the show closed in the spring, it was clear to everyone that they were no longer a couple.

L'Engle did not try to talk to Franklin until the day she heard that President Franklin Delano Roosevelt had died. Franklin was a great admirer of the president. She called him. They talked for a while and began to date again sporadically after that. They saw each other a couple of times in the summer and once in the fall when Franklin was on break from a play. He sent her flowers for her birthday in November. He later came over to see her and asked her to marry him.

L'Engle called her mother, who had just left New York after a month-long visit. She was quite surprised. A few weeks later, L'Engle threw a party at her apartment. Franklin hid in the kitchen. When he came out to greet everyone, they were all surprised. The additional news that they were going to get married was astonishing.

One of the actresses in Franklin's play left, and L'Engle was cast in her place. The play was *The Joyous Season*, and the two left on tour together. While the play was in Chicago, they decided to look for an Episcopal church. They met with the rector, and the following Saturday—January 26, 1946—they were married. Two of their friends attended, and they all had lunch afterward. They had to return to work immediately, so after lunch, the four went back to the theater. That day they had both a matinee and an evening performance. A few days after the wedding, the couple rented a car and visited their family. In Jacksonville, Florida, L'Engle's mother threw a party for them. It was ironic that L'Engle, the girl who had gone on arranged dates and was not socially inclined, had married a charming and handsome actor with no help from anyone.

Names had always been important to L'Engle, so when she married, she wanted to change her name to Franklin. Her publishing house advised her not to do so. She was a known writer with the name L'Engle, and they did not want her to change it. Her husband agreed.

BUYING CROSSWICKS

After their wedding, she and Franklin bought a house in Connecticut. L'Engle's mother named it Crosswicks, after the village where L'Engle's father lived in New Jersey. L'Engle also had her second book, *Ilsa*, published. The following June, she gave birth to the couple's first child, Josephine. L'Engle and Franklin had not intended to have children so soon, but an accident changed their minds. Franklin was driving home with a friend. He was speeding, and a bee flew into the car. He tried to shoo the insect out, but was unable to. Finally, he slowed down to about 20 miles per hour so that it could fly out. Just then, one of the car's tires blew out. If he had not slowed down, the accident could have been fatal. His narrow brush with death convinced L'Engle and Franklin to start having children right away.

L'Engle was determined to stay home and take care of her daughter herself. She stopped acting, but she did not stop writing. Money was tight. "My second novel had been published to distinguished reviews but very modest sales, and I was running out of *The Small Rain* money,"[5] L'Engle wrote in *Two-Part Invention.* Franklin left for long periods to work in plays. On the day their daughter was born, he had to work. He took his wife to the hospital in the morning and then had to leave for two performances.

Franklin continued his work in theater while L'Engle stayed home, raised their daughter, and wrote new stories. In 1949, *And Both Were Young* was published. In 1951, another book, *Camilla Dickinson*, was published.

L'Engle was determined that her daughter should have a different upbringing than she had. There was no nanny to care for Josephine. There were no dinners alone. In fact, because Franklin kept late hours as an actor in the theater, L'Engle would put her daughter to bed early, then, when Franklin got home in the middle of the night, she would wake Josephine up to play with him. Josephine went back to bed when her parents did, very late at night.

Things were going well for the family, but Franklin and L'Engle decided that they wanted to raise their children away from New York City. Though they had initially used Crosswicks as their summer home, they decided to live there year round. Early in 1952, they made the move. Shortly thereafter, in March, their son, Bion, was born. Bion was named after L'Engle's grandfather, Bion Barnett.

Because the commute to New York City's theater district was too long, Franklin had to give up working there. At first, he tried to find work in neighboring towns, but he was told that he was too qualified for blue-collar work. Because their town had no grocery store, the couple found a run-down general store in the middle of town that also housed the post office. They took it over and ran the store for the next nine years.

The next addition to the Franklin family happened suddenly. One day, while L'Engle was at home listening to the record player, her friend Liz called to say that her husband had died. Liz left her daughter, Maria, at Crosswicks for a month while she got things in order. At the end of the summer, Liz asked L'Engle if she would take care of Maria if anything happened to her. That November, something did. Liz fell ill suddenly during a rehearsal for a play, and by the next morning, she had passed away. The Franklins adopted seven-year-old Maria. It was 1956.

With the old house, the general store, and three young children to look after, there was not much time for L'Engle to write. After she took care of the household's needs, made dinner, and put the kids to bed, she tried to write, but she was so tired that she sometimes fell asleep with her head on the typewriter. It was not until 1957 that she published another book, *A Winter's Love.* It had been six years since her last published work. Her work always met with good reviews, and, though the sales were good to moderate, it was enough to make her an established writer. She then began work on *Meet the Austins*, her first novel marketed to young adults. Her biggest successes were still to come.

Madeleine L'Engle and Hugh Franklin at the time of their marriage in 1946. Having met while working together in the theater, the couple understood the need to balance their professional lives with their family life, which eventually included their children, Josephine, Bion, and Maria.

3

A Rough Road for *Wrinkle*

MADELEINE, SCIENTIST

With the publication of *A Winter's Love* in 1957, L'Engle had returned to publishing. In *A Circle of Quiet*, she described how being a mother of young children made it impossible to be dedicated to her writing: "During the long drag of years before our youngest child went to school, my love for my family and my need to write were in acute conflict. The problem was really that I put two things first. My husband and children came first. So did my writing. Bump."[1] She wished she lived on a desert island, with all the time in the world to write.

She decided that she would write at night when the children were asleep. Franklin would get up early in the morning and take care of breakfast so that she could sleep late. By the end of the 1950s, her children were all in school, and she did not need to keep such late nights anymore. She finally had the time and silence she needed to write. At the same time, Franklin felt that he needed to move on from the store. He returned to acting and worked in New York, commuting back to Crosswicks when he could. Eventually, they decided to move back to New York so that the family could all be together. While they were searching for an apartment toward the end of 1959, they spent their weekends in a hotel. Josephine found an ad for a luxury apartment. There was no price, and L'Engle was sure they would never be able to afford it. Josephine insisted they go look.

The apartment had eight rooms, four baths, and fourteen closets. The rent was $128 a month. The apartment was not really a luxury apartment, but it was large, and in a rent-controlled building, which meant the rent would remain steadily low for a long time. It was perfect for the family. They signed the lease the next day, and moved in on February 1, 1960. L'Engle found nearby schools, St. Hilda's and St. Hugh's, for the children to attend. Since Hugh was Franklin's first name, they took this as a good omen.

During this time, the manuscript for *Meet the Austins* was making the rounds to publishing houses but was met with rejection everywhere. L'Engle believed that publishers had difficulty with the book because it began with a death. At that time, deaths in children's literature were almost unheard of. Even though traditional children's stories like the fairy tales made popular by the Brothers Grimm and Hans Christian Andersen often contained elements of death, by the 1950s most fairy tales had been rewritten to exclude themes that were thought to be too violent for children. For example, the original version of the children's classic *Little Red Riding Hood* described the grandmother and the child being eaten and the woodsman hunting the wolf for its skin. Recent versions changed the story so that the wolf simply shut the grandmother in a closet, and Little Red Riding Hood was never harmed.

With her manuscript, L'Engle was fighting an uphill battle against this gentler trend in children's writing. However, her writing was simply reflecting what was going on in her life and she could not have changed it even if she wanted to. In the span of two years, four close family friends had died and she "really wasn't finding the answers to [her] big questions in the logical places."[2] She turned to physics. At the time, L'Engle was completely unfamiliar with science. She told an interviewer at *Booklist* that in college, she avoided science as much as possible. To fulfill her science requirement, she chose psychology, which was "as far from science as [she] could get and still fill the requirement."[3] She chose books by the physicist Albert Einstein. She was fascinated by his theory of special relativity, "which applies to objects moving at constant speed," and general relativity, "which covers accelerating things and explains how gravity works."[4] She also found that she and Einstein shared an interest in science that went hand in hand with their faith. On the Random House Web site, she recalled, "I read a book of Einstein's, in which he said that anyone who's not lost in rapturous awe

A 1947 photo of the famed theoretical physicist Albert Einstein (1879–1955), who is best known for his theory of relativity. Einstein's work inspired L'Engle to explore both science and the nature of faith.

at the power and glory of the mind behind the universe is as good as a burnt-out candle."[5] She felt that she had found someone who really understood the nature of the universe and the nature of faith.

At the time, L'Engle was asking what she called "big theological questions." She spoke to her ministers at the church in Connecticut. They tried to answer her questions. They also told her to read German theologians. She said that these books put her to sleep; they did not help her. "So I kept on thinking and asking my questions. Eventually, I started asking my questions of the stars. . . . I began to read astronomers and physicists."[6]

She continued to read Einstein as well as Max Planck's quantum mechanics. Planck was also a physicist. He worked on a quantum theory that is the basis of chemistry, mathematics, and physics. L'Engle felt that these physicists' ideas about the universe were better than any ideas she had found in religious books. She began to read more of Einstein and Planck's theories as well as texts dealing with cosmology, or the study of the universe. This was her serious reading. For enjoyment, she typically read English women mystery writers, because she felt that they "have a sense of what the human soul is about and why people do dark and terrible things."[7] She thought of science, literature, art, and theology as all part of the same language that tries to uncover the mystery of the universe. All of these themes about the nature of the universe, mystery, and the idea of people doing bad things all wound up in the manuscript for *A Wrinkle in Time*. She later described that book as her "rebuttal to the German theologians."[8] In 1960, *Meet the Austins* was finally published by Vanguard. By that time, the manuscript for *A Wrinkle in Time* was ready for submission, and her agent began to send it around.

WHERE *WRINKLE* CAME FROM

L'Engle said that the idea for *A Wrinkle in Time* simply came to her when the family decided it was time to move back to the city. Franklin was no longer happy running the general store, and he wanted to get back to acting. The family decided to take a cross-country trip and then find an apartment in New York City. Along the way, Franklin got word that he was wanted for a Broadway play, so they hurried back to the city. On the drive back, "the names, *Mrs Whatsit, Mrs Who and Mrs Which"* popped into her head. She turned around and told her children, "Hey kids, listen to these three great names that just popped into my mind; I'll have to write a book about them."[9] As L'Engle described in *Horn Book,* she felt compelled to write the story: "I think that fantasy must possess the author and simply use him. . . . I can't possibly tell you how I came to write it. It was simply a book I had to write. I had no choice. And it was only *after* it was written that I realized what some of it meant."[10] When she had finished writing the book, there was the problem of finding a title for it. Her mother was staying at their home in Crosswicks at the

Did you know...

In 1999, *Time* magazine's editors produced several lists of the century's best, from children's books to films to music albums. L'Engle's *A Wrinkle in Time* lost to *Charlotte's Web,* written by E.B. White, but the book had good company. The other runner-up was *The Chronicles of Narnia* by C.S. Lewis.

time, and, after a night of insomnia, L'Engle thought her mother might need a cup of coffee. When L'Engle took it in, her mother told her that she had a title for the book; she said that it was right out of the text. L'Engle thought the title was perfect.

A 2005 review by Barbara Talcroft for the Web site *Children's Literature* describes *A Wrinkle in Time* as "a work of fantasy and fiction with some Christian theology."[11] The main character, Meg Murry, along with a school friend, Calvin, travel through a wrinkle in time, called a tesseract, to an alternate dimension and another planet. They do this to rescue Meg's father who has disappeared while doing a secret assignment for the government. The characters encounter transcendental beings that help them as they travel through folds in the fabric of time. These beings reveal that the galaxy is being overtaken by the embodiment of evil, a being called IT. IT is a disembodied brain with telepathic powers. It controls the inhabitants of planets by taking away their free will and individualism.

Editors did not seem to know how to categorize the story. First of all, it was a science fiction story with a female main character, which one did not find before *Wrinkle.* After this book was published, a new genre name, science fantasy, was developed. L'Engle said that the category science fantasy is "probably a better description than either fantasy or science fiction for my books."[12] The book also contained difficult themes. For editors, the main problem was that the book dealt primarily with the idea of evil. They felt that the themes were too difficult for children. Others could not figure out if it was a book for children or for adults. Then there were the science and Christian elements. "It's based on Einstein's theory of relativity and Planck's quantum theory. It's good solid science, but also its good, solid theology," L'Engle said in a 1986 interview with the *National Catholic Reporter.* Needless to say, the book was a hard sell.

Despite having published six books, L'Engle was not at that point the kind of author who publishers worked hard to impress. Her manuscripts were not always given the attention they deserved. Because hundreds of manuscripts are sent to publishers every week, senior editors cannot possibly read each one. Instead, a junior editor, or a college intern, reads the manuscripts that come in. The manuscripts are placed in something called the "slush pile" before they are read. If an intern or junior editor finds something that they like, only then does it get passed on to a senior editor. All editors know that good books are sometimes mistakenly rejected because of this method, and L'Engle knew this, too. She also understood, however, that there was no real solution to that problem. She was still upset that, even as a previously published author, her work was only read by senior editors in about half of the publishing houses it was sent to.

Every major publisher at the time turned down *Wrinkle.* After two years, L'Engle had 26 rejection letters to show for her work. Most editors said that they loved the story, but they did not think that children would understand it. L'Engle found this amusing. She knew that children would understand her work perfectly well, and that it was the grown-ups who did not.

Nevertheless, the rejections were taking a toll on L'Engle, who wanted her book to be a success. Having her work published mattered a great deal to her. With so many rejections, she once again considered giving up. In a 1998 *Booklist* interview, she said that, at the time, she could not have imagined that the book would have become a children's classic. She said, "I called it hack and said, 'Let's just quit.'" However, she kept submitting the same manuscript because she "thought it was good." In fact, she felt it was her best work.

TAKING A CHANCE

One of her last rejection letters arrived on the Monday before Christmas. L'Engle was wrapping Christmas presents and trying to pretend that she was not bothered by the bad news. Later she found out that she had mixed up the presents. She had sent perfume to a single man and a tie to a teenaged girl. Disappointed by the rejection, she called her agent and asked to have the manuscript back. He refused at first, but finally agreed to send it back to her; she was finished trying to find a publisher for it.

After Christmas, L'Engle threw a small party for her mother's friends. One of them offered to introduce her to John Farrar of the publishing house Farrar, Straus, as it was then called. L'Engle did not want anything to do with publishers, but took the train into New York City to meet him anyway. She said that when she handed him the manuscript, he was very kind and warm. He had read some of her work before and told her that he liked it very much. Then he asked what she was working on. She explained about *A Wrinkle in Time* and told him that she liked it, but nobody else did, or, if they did like it, they were afraid to publish it. She left the manuscript with him. Two weeks later, she signed a contract for the book over lunch with John Farrar and Hal Vursell, an editor at

Farrar, Straus. The two men agreed to publish the story, but they told her not to be disappointed if it didn't do well. They said that they were publishing it because they loved it, not because they thought it would make money. At the time, Farrar, Straus did not publish stories for children and young adults. L'Engle insisted that *A Wrinkle in Time* was a book for children, so they published it as juvenile fiction. *Wrinkle* set the stage for Farrar, Straus to publish other children's books.

In *A Circle of Quiet*, L'Engle quoted an interview by Hal Vursell, who described why editors might not have wanted to publish the story:

> We have all, from time to time, chosen and published obviously superior books . . . only to have that very book stillborn. Now editors have emotions, too, and when this happens, believe it or not, they bleed. . . . So to have refused *A Wrinkle in Time* carries no stigma of editorial cowardice; the bravest of us pause from time to time to bind up our wounds. It was our own good fortune that the manuscript reached us at a moment when we were ready to do battle again.[13]

L'Engle's relationship with the publishing house Farrar, Straus and Giroux (as it later became known) continued on through many successful books. They published the three sequels to *A Wrinkle in Time*, now known as the "Time Fantasy" series or the "Time Quartet," as well as the four sequels to *Meet the Austins*, also known as the "Austin Family" series. In 1981, *A Ring of Endless Light,* the fifth story in the "Austin Family" series, was a Newbery Honor book. Early in her writing career, L'Engle realized that many publishers were unwilling to take risks with their writers. They often wanted them to write the same kind of story over and over again. L'Engle credited

Farrar, Straus and Giroux with allowing her to experiment with her writing, which she said was essential to a writer who wants to grow.

A photo of Madeleine L'Engle as a successful author.* A Wrinkle in Time, *which had been rejected by numerous publishing houses, cemented her reputation as a serious writer. The novel not only won the Newbery Award but also earned L'Engle legions of fans.

4

Afraid of Camazotz

WHAT'S IT REALLY ABOUT?

Farrar, Straus and Giroux was ready to do battle for *A Wrinkle in Time,* but they did not have to worry much. There were minor battles to be waged for the book, but, overwhelmingly, everyone loved it. The first minor battle was with L'Engle herself. She had specifically taken out the periods after each "Mrs" of Mrs Which, Whatsit, and Who. She felt that this was important because they needed to be distinguished as extraterrestrial beings. Unfortunately, the copy editor at her publisher did not know that was on purpose. The copy editor is the person who corrects all the punctuation and grammar mistakes in a book before it is printed. By the time L'Engle made the discovery, it was too late to fix the error, as it would have been very expensive to make the change. L'Engle decided to live with the mistake. When the book was ready to be published in England, L'Engle made sure that the periods were taken out. Unfortunately, the publisher in England also took out the periods after the Mr. and Mrs. for Mr. and Mrs. Murry.

When the book hit the market at first, everything seemed to be smooth sailing. The reviews were good, but the reader response was *phenomenal.* So many editors had turned down the manuscript thinking that kids wouldn't get it. Kids not only "got it"—they loved it.

The book begins with the line, "It was a dark and stormy night," which is the first line of another famous novel, *Paul Clifford*, by Edward George Bulwer-Lytton. This opening line later became famous in the *Peanuts* comic strip by Charles M. Schulz. Snoopy wanted to be a writer, and he always began his novels with this classic first line.

Wrinkle's heroine is Meg Murry, who is wrongly regarded as an underachiever by her teachers. Her mother is a beautiful scientist who still manages to get dinner on the table. Her father is a brilliant mathematician who has mysteriously disappeared. She has 10-year-old twin brothers, who are great at sports, and a younger brother, who is a genius, though most people think of him as odd. What begins in a typical house, with a slightly unusual family, soon becomes a fantastic tale. A being called Mrs Whatsit appears and leads Meg and Charles Wallace, her youngest brother, on a quest to save their father from an evil that is taking over the universe. The two children team up with a popular boy from school, Calvin O'Keefe, who also has extraordinary powers, and they band together to battle the evil called IT, an evil that is trying to make everything and everyone the same. As Meg says, "Like and equal are not the same thing at all!"[1] It becomes up to Meg to save Charles Wallace, whose mind has been taken over by IT.

CUTTING-EDGE SCIENCE

A Wrinkle in Time was written before the explosion of technology that we have today. In 1962, there were no cell phones, personal computers, or video games. No one had stepped on the moon. There was no Mars rover, satellites, space shuttle, or International Space Station. It was written before the television and movie science fiction classics *Star Wars* and *Star Trek.* In her introduction to the novel, Lisa Sonne wrote,

> Throughout *A Wrinkle in Time,* the universe is in a struggle with the Black Thing. L'Engle wrote of the Black Thing before astronomers found black holes, which suck up everything around them, and long before scientists announced that almost all of our universe is composed of invisible "dark

Did you know...

Throughout her life, L'Engle remained dedicated to education. In the summers of 1965, 1966, and 1971, she was a member of the faculty of the University of Indiana at Bloomington. She lectured for many years at Wheaton College in Illinois, beginning in 1976. She became the writer-in-residence at Ohio State University in Ohio in 1970 and the University of Rochester in New York in 1972.

matter" and "dark energy," which science knows almost nothing about.[2]

The children travel through multiple dimensions on their quest. At the time of her writing, there were only three known physical dimensions—length, width, and height. Today, science is uncovering numerous other dimensions, including time. L'Engle was careful to do a lot of science research before writing *Wrinkle,* but there were things that she could not include because they had not been discovered yet. When Meg's father asks her to recite the elements of the periodic table to escape the hold of IT, she does not mention rutherfordium, meitnerium, darmstadtium, or roentgenium, because they were discovered after the book was written. One of L'Engle's points in writing this book was that there is still so much to discover. She was quite right, and, more than 40 years later, there is still even more to discover.

In addition to being remarkable for its foresight into science and technology, *Wrinkle* is also about something fairly normal: individuality. L'Engle had struggled with this issue for years as a child, dealing with teachers who did not understand her and who referred to her by a number instead of by name. *Wrinkle* was about overcoming that. L'Engle believed that we are still fighting conformity today. It is in the way everyone dresses alike and listens to the same music and in peer pressure. She believed that the problems in the book are still very much alive. "Just look out the window," L'Engle told Suzanne Macneille. "It's still going on."[3] There is no question that Meg, who is misunderstood by her teachers and her peers, is really L'Engle. "Every single one of my adolescent heroines is based on my own experience,"[4] she wrote.

Meg, like L'Engle, felt lost and alone. She, too, had a great talent to discover in herself. For *The Hero Project* (2006), a young interviewer asked L'Engle about the similarities between herself and the character Meg. "Well, anything anyone writes is autobiographical," she said. "The main thing is my teachers thought I was stupid."[5] Meg is not the only character based on a real-life person that appears in her books. Charles Wallace is based on her son, Bion. The character's name, Charles Wallace, combines the first names of her father, Charles Camp, and her father-in-law, Wallace Franklin.

The book was also written during a time in L'Engle's life when she was looking for a safe haven for her family. The world at the time seemed to be on the brink of a nuclear war. "We had a feeling of imminent disaster—but we tried anyway, for the children, to create that safe place," she recalled. "I was conscious of creating it in life, and the books were echoing what that life was like."[6]

People have described the book as science fiction or science fantasy. L'Engle felt that the book defied classification because there was no such thing as science fantasy when it was written. The term came later. Some describe the book as a religious tale. Others think it is anti-Christian. She told the interviewer for *The Hero Project*,

> When that book was first published . . . in 1962, it was discovered by the evangelical world as a Christian book. Now not one word of that book has changed. What has changed? Why are people turning on something that they affirmed? And the question is why has so much fear, so much anger, come into the world?[7]

A photo of schoolchildren during a "duck and cover" drill in the 1950s. These drills were common during the Cold War, when many people feared nuclear war was very possible. Such fears inspired L'Engle to create a "safe haven" for her children in her books.

A RELIGIOUS BATTLE

A Wrinkle in Time is one of the 10 most banned books in the United States. It is on the list with such classics as *The Grapes of Wrath* by John Steinbeck and *The Diary of a Young Girl* by Anne Frank. These two happened to be among L'Engle's favorite books. As of this writing, *A Wrinkle in Time* is on the American Library Association's list of the 100 Most Frequently Challenged Books, at number 22.

The religious content in the story is not hidden. When the children name people on Earth who are fighting against the evil entity, the names include Jesus, Buddha, and Gandhi. Jesus was the founder of Christianity, Buddha started the Buddhist religion, and Gandhi was a spiritual leader in India. The characters also quote passages from the Bible. The Mrs W's are former stars, but they act like guardian angels.

In *A Sense of Story: Essays on Contemporary Writers for Children,* John Rowland Townsend writes that in *Wrinkle* "the clash of good and evil is at a cosmic level. . . . Here evil is obviously the reduction of people to a mindless mass, while good is individuality, art, and love."[8]

WINNING!

Regardless of how some view the book, thousands of new fans discover it every year. One year, a teacher wrote to L'Engle to tell her about the students in her class who had read and loved the book. L'Engle thought the letter was moving. She was touched by the teacher's love and dedication particularly since the instructor taught a class of mentally disabled children who had had *A Wrinkle in Time* read aloud to them. They also sent letters to her. The teacher apologized for their handwriting, and spelling and grammar mistakes, but this did not matter to L'Engle. She marveled at how they were able to express their love in their writing.

Besides the readers, the critics also loved the story. In 1963, L'Engle got a phone call that a lot of people have asked her about. It was from the Newbery Committee.

> It's a moment I couldn't possibly forget. It was in the morning, just as I was hurrying the children off to school. My husband, who was in a play on Broadway, was asleep, and if there's an unbreakable rule in our household, it is that we do not wake Daddy up in the morning, and we don't speak to him until after he's had two cups of coffee, read the paper, and done his crossword puzzle.
>
> The telephone rang. It was long distance, and an impossible connection. I couldn't hear anything. The operator told me to hang up and she'd try again. The long-distance phone ringing unexpectedly always makes me nervous: is something wrong with one of the grandparents? The phone rang again, and still the connection was full of static and roaring, so the operator told me to hang up and she'd try once more. This time I could barely hear a voice: "This is Ruth Gagliardo, of the Newbery-Caldecott committee." There was a pause, and she asked, "Can you hear me?" "Yes, I can hear you." Then she told me that *Wrinkle* had won the medal. My response was an inarticulate squawk; Ruth told me later that it was a special pleasure to her to have me *that* excited.
>
> We hung up, and I flew through the dining room and the living room like a winged giraffe, burst upon the bedroom door, flew in, gave a great leap, and landed on the bed on top of my startled husband.
>
> Joy![9]

One result of her success was that she made many more friends than she would have if she had not won. The award also allowed her to travel around the country and lecture. Just after *Wrinkle* won the Newbery, L'Engle was invited to parties thrown for and by people in the literature community. She met a lot of publishers who said that they wished she had sent the manuscript for the book to them. She informed them that she had, in fact, done so. At one party, someone whose publishing company had rejected the story approached L'Engle. He refused to believe that his publishing house had rejected something so good. L'Engle went to her journal and found the page where she wrote down how upset she was on the day that she got the rejection from his publishing house. He bemoaned that he had never seen the manuscript. He was sure he would not have rejected it if he had.

A Wrinkle in Time is about discovery. It is about scientific discovery and personal discovery. More than 40 years after its first publication, the book is still being discovered by new readers. In a 2005 review of the book, a critic wrote that although many scientific concepts in the book "were conceived since the book's 1962 publication . . . [they] are amazingly applicable . . . and help to ensure that this imaginative book will be read for a long time into the future."[10]

In addition to the Newbery, the book was awarded the Sequoyah Book Award and the Lewis Carroll Shelf Award in 1963. It was also a runner-up for the Hans Christian Andersen Award.

Above, Hugh Franklin in his long-running role of Dr. Charles Tyler on the ABC television soap opera, All My Children. *Pictured with him is costar Ruth Warrick, who played Phoebe Wallingford.*

5

Body of Work

A Wrinkle in Time made L'Engle a major writer—not only an award-winner, but well paid and wildly famous. The soaring sales of *Wrinkle* allowed her to write without worrying about finding a supplemental job. Franklin's work in the theater was going well, and he later moved to television. For many years, he played Dr. Charles Tyler on the daytime soap opera *All My Children.* L'Engle and Franklin were both flourishing in their careers. Occasionally, the two worked together to give lectures. Mostly, they enjoyed having careers that had nothing to do with one another. While Franklin became a famous soap star, L'Engle wrote prolifically over the next 40-plus years.

THE AUSTINS

L'Engle's body of work forms an interconnected web, where the families and friends of various characters are followed throughout their lifetimes. Often, secondary characters in one book go on to star in their own stories in subsequent books. Her official Web site, www.madeleinelengle.com, lists 63 books by the author, many of which are part of a series. One of her most popular series is about the Austin family.

Vicky Austin, the eldest girl in a family of four children, narrates *Meet the Austins*, the first book in the series. John is the eldest of the children. Suzy and Rob are the youngest. The main problem in the book is the adoption of Maggy, a bratty girl who disrupts the Austin kids' happy life. Eventually, Maggy learns to be a part of the family, and the other children accept her. The story was written while L'Engle and Franklin were still living at Crosswicks, around the time that they adopted their daughter Maria. Though L'Engle never says that Maggy is based on Maria, or the time that she was adopted, the similarities make it very likely. However, she is very clear about the character Rob. "Rob Austin [is simply] our youngest child, and there's nothing I can do about it."[1]

In 1963, *The Moon by Night* was published. A now 14-year-old Vicky is having what her family calls a "difficult" year. Her year becomes even more complicated when Zachary and Andy come into her life during a cross-country trip. The trip takes the family from the Atlantic coast to the Pacific coast. Over the course of the vacation, Vicky learns about love and friendship.

A year later, L'Engle took the Austin family back in time to tell the story of a seven-year-old Vicky Austin in *The*

Twenty-Four Days Before Christmas. In this story, Vicky is preparing for the Christmas pageant. She is worried because her mother, who is pregnant, might have to go to the hospital to have the baby during Christmas.

In L'Engle's 1968 novel, *The Young Unicorns*, the story is less about Vicky and more about L'Engle's classic theme of good triumphing over evil. In it, she introduces new characters: Emily, who is blind and sometimes stays with the Austins, and Dave, who reads to Emily.

Seventeen years after *The Moon by Night,* L'Engle wrote *A Ring of Endless Light*. It picks up Vicky's story just after *The Moon by Night*. She is now 16 years old, and the Austin family is spending the summer taking care of their dying grandfather. Over the course of the summer, Vicky finds herself entwined in the lives of different men: her grandfather, who gives her advice whenever he is well enough; Zachary, who has followed her from the previous story; and her brother's friend Adam, whom Vicky seems to be interested in romantically. She also tries to comfort Leo, the son of the man who lost his own life while trying to save Zachary. In addition to dealing with the people in her life, Vicky discovers something amazing about herself. While working with Adam at a marine biology station, Vicky discovers that she is telepathic.

A Ring of Endless Light was named a Newbery Honor Book in 1980. It won the Dorothy Canfield Fisher Children's Book Award and the California Young Reader Medal in 1982. In 1983, it won the Colorado Children's Book Award.

In *Troubling a Star,* published in 1987, Vicky travels to Antarctica. She is going to visit Adam, a college student on a biology expedition. Vicky is excited to go, but her excitement is dampened when she receives notes of warning. "When she embarks on her journey, danger indeed seems to lurk around every corner," a *Publishers Weekly* reviewer noted, going on to say that L'Engle's "stunning descriptions of the Antarctic waters and their inhabitants transmit a strong ecological message."[2] A reviewer from *School Library Journal* also found the descriptions of the wildlife and Antarctic habitats "lively" but the plot lacking. "The mystery itself is fairly transparent, even predictable."[3]

L'Engle wrote a second Austin family Christmas story. *A Full House: An Austin Family Christmas* was published in 1999. In this story, yet another woman is expecting a baby. This time, it is a visitor staying with the family.

TIME FANTASY

A Wrinkle in Time was the first in the "Time Fantasy" series. In this series, the characters travel back and forth through time and dimensions. The series also makes a departure from L'Engle's stories based in "chronos," or real time. These stories are told in "kairos." Kairos is a Greek word that means "a time when conditions are right for the accomplishment of a crucial action: the opportune and decisive moment."[4] In theology, the word is used to describe a time that is determined by God's purpose. Many of L'Engle's books are categorized by chronos and kairos.

Although *Wrinkle* was met with critical acclaim and hordes of fans, L'Engle did not write a sequel to the story until 1973—11 years after the first book was published. *A Wind in the Door* follows Meg and Charles Wallace on another fantasy adventure. This time, Charles Wallace announces that he has seen dragons in the vegetable garden. Meg, Calvin, and Charles Wallace join the dragon on a trip into space, to battle evil once again. The evil this time is called the Echthroi. The children learn that even the tiniest things can have a huge impact on the universe. Karin Snelson, in a review for Amazon.com, called it "masterful" and said that L'Engle "jumps seamlessly from a child's world . . . to deeply sinister, cosmic battles between good and evil."[5]

In 1978, L'Engle completed the "Time Fantasy" series with *A Swiftly Tilting Planet*, which won the American Book Award. In this novel, we meet a 15-year-old Charles Wallace who must travel back in time to change history. With the help of a unicorn and a type of telepathic communication called kything, he has to save the world once again. This time, the characters are trying to avoid a nuclear conflict. Emilie Coulter, writing for Amazon.com, remarked: "L'Engle kindles the intellect, inspiring young

Did you know...

Names have always been important to L'Engle. In her family line, there are at least four Madeleines: L'Engle's great-grandmother, who was nicknamed Mado; L'Engle's mother; the author herself; and her granddaughter, nicknamed Lena. Lena is sometimes listed as Lena and other times with an accent, as Léna.

people to ask questions of the world and learn by challenging."[6] Cindy Lombardo, writing for *School Library Journal*, said that the audio recording of the book, narrated by L'Engle herself, "detracts from the quality of the listening experience," that, though the material is "wonderful," it would have been better if "presented by a professional narrator rather than by the author."[7]

Published in 1986, *Many Waters* follows the twins Sandy and Dennys Murry, who are now 15. By accident, they travel back to the time of Noah, before the Great Flood of the Bible story. In this story, angels walk the earth and unicorns exist. Christine Berman remarked in *School Library Journal*, "[T]he strength of this book lies in its haunting descriptions of a time resonant of our own. Its weakness is a pat ending and characters so slightly drawn that we hardly care."[8]

An Acceptable Time was published three years later. It is about Polly O'Keefe, the daughter of Calvin and Meg Murry. She is suddenly dropped through a time gate to a prehistoric era, 3,000 years ago, and is left in the midst of a group of people who believe in human sacrifice. A reviewer for *VOYA* (*Voice of Youth Advocates*) library magazine wrote: "L'Engle has again achieved the award-winning style of *A Wrinkle in Time.*"[9]

In *A Circle of Quiet,* L'Engle said that she was thinking about doing another story about Meg that happens when the character is in her 50s.

OTHER WORKS

Along with her fiction for young adults, L'Engle has written books for adult audiences. Her autobiographies are collectively called the Crosswicks Journals because they were all written during summers at Crosswicks. They are *A Circle of Quiet* (1972), *The Summer of the Great-Grandmother* (1974), *The Irrational Season* (1977), and *Two-Part Invention: The Story of a Marriage* (1988). They offer readers a complete view into L'Engle's life, both professionally and personally. In addition to her journals, L'Engle wrote many articles and several plays. One of her plays, *18 Washington Square, South: A Comedy in One Act*, was first produced in Northampton, Massachusetts in 1940, while L'Engle was still pursuing her acting career. Nine years later, she wrote *How Now Brown Cow* with Robert Hartung for production in New York. *The Journey with Jonah,* another one-act play, was produced in New York in 1970. Three years earlier, in 1967, an edition was published with illustrations by Leonard Everett Fisher.

L'Engle has also published collections of poetry. The first, *Lines Scribbled on an Envelope*, was published in 1969, followed by *The Risk of Birth* in 1974. Four years later, *The Weather of the Heart* was published. L'Engle's official Web site describes this book as written by "a poet who is in touch with God, man, and the universal weather."[10] In it, L'Engle attempts to chart the weather within the human heart. In 1987, *A Cry like a Bell* was published, and, in 1996, L'Engle worked with her longtime friend Luci Shaw to write *Wintersong*, a book of Christmas readings.

While many of L'Engle's books have been made into audio books, some have also had other media adaptations. Three of her books have been made into audiocassettes with

*A photo of Madeleine L'Engle (*right*) taken during a performance of her play* 18 Washington Square South *in 1940.*

filmstrips: *A Wrinkle in Time, A Wind in the Door*, and *A Ring of Endless Light.* Four have been made into talking books: *A Wrinkle in Time, A Wind in the Door, Dragons in the Waters, Camilla*, and *The Arm of the Starfish.* Some of L'Engle's books have also been adapted for the media on a grand scale.

Above, a photo of the actor Gregory Smith, who starred in the 2003 film adaptation of* A Wrinkle in Time*, directed by John Kent Harrison. L'Engle claimed not to have seen much of the movie—and was not particularly pleased by what she saw.

6

Going Hollywood

A YOUNG FAN

As a young girl, Catherine Hand read *A Wrinkle in Time* and fell in love with the story. "I took out a piece of paper and a pen and started a letter to Walt Disney," she recalled. "I wanted to tell him about this book and have him star me as Meg." Then she stopped. "And then I was concerned that Mr. Disney might not get it right. So I thought, 'God, I've got to grow up and make it myself.' "[1] She did, but it wasn't easy. There were obstacles around every corner. She had to struggle, much like the main character, Meg. Except, she was not struggling against evil, she struggled against other fans who wanted to film the book, too.

Hand's first obstacle was L'Engle herself. At first, L'Engle did not want the book made into a movie. She wanted to make sure that the movie would be "a faithful adaptation of the book," Hand said in an interview with Nick Rafeal for the *Boston Globe*. It took Hand 20 years to get the deal made. When the deal was struck, L'Engle herself was not involved. Her granddaughter, Charlotte Jones, took her place. How did Hand get L'Engle to agree to it? She made friends with the author and read every screenplay herself. She waited until she found the right script that did the book justice. Finding the right adaptation of the story was important to Hand.

Just as the book speaks to readers on many levels, Hand realized the script needed to do the same. As a young girl, Hand felt that the heroine, Meg, spoke to her. She still believes that the female hero is important for girls today. "One of the most unique things about this story is that it is a mythic quest from the perspective of a young girl."[2] In a culture where the young girl is usually the damsel in distress who is saved from the dragon, Hand felt that Meg was different and important. She likens Meg to Luke Skywalker in *Star Wars* or Dorothy of *The Wizard of Oz*. In the end, these characters are all trying to make something in their world better. It is the same with Meg.

Susan Shilliday was chosen to write the script for the film adaptation. Her first problem was figuring out how to handle all of the abstract concepts on film. "What is a tesseract?" Shilliday asked herself. "How do you handle that on film?" The problem is that the book has as much to do with inner struggle and abstract images as it does with scenery. It was difficult to translate that into a stream of images that could be captured by a camera.

John Kent Harrison was brought on to direct the movie. He was having the same problem with finding the right way to handle the images. Harrison said, "I found the book to be an inspirational work rather than a great narrative book." Can inspiration be filmed? The answer was to use special effects.

Even the special effects proved to be daunting. Since movies like *Star Wars* and other science fiction films, with their stunning visual effects, the movie audience was extremely sophisticated. *Wrinkle* had been written in the 1960s, when that kind of movie technology did not exist. Those working on the movie had to find a convincing way to show tesseracts and the evil brain, IT. Everyone was worried about what the fans would think because, of course, "a big static brain just isn't the same on the screen as it is on the page," Shilliday said. In most cases, the producers and scriptwriters would have rearranged the narrative a little to accommodate the movie. Because this book is a beloved

Did you know...

The Academy of Science Fiction, Fantasy and Horror Films nominated the television movie, *A Wrinkle in Time*, for a Saturn Award for "Best DVD Television Programming" in 2005. That same year, the Writers Guild of America nominated Susan Shilliday in the category of "Children's Script" to recognize her work in writing the screenplay for *A Wrinkle in Time*.

***A portrait of Madeleine L'Engle at age 15, about the same age as her character Meg in* A Wrinkle in Time.**

classic, however, they did not feel they had the license to do that.

Everyone who worked on the movie had ideas of how they wanted to see it on film, and everyone's ideas were different. L'Engle understood this. As a writer, she believed that a work of art is a collaboration between the writer and the reader. Readers bring something different to the story because of how they read it. When the movie was released in 2001, it was first presented as a mini-series with a more than four-hour run time. It was broadcast in Canada, Australia, and Germany. In 2003, the movie was re-shot and re-edited into a movie-length film of about two hours. It won the best feature film award at the Toronto International Film Festival for Children. The new version of the movie was aired on ABC in 2004.

The part of Meg went to Katie Stuart, who had been in *X2: X-Men United*. David Dorfman played Charles Wallace; Gregory Smith, of the television series *Everwood*, played Calvin O'Keefe; and Alison Elliott, Kate Nelligan, and Alfre Woodard, respectively, played the celestial guides, Mrs Who, Mrs Which, and Mrs Whatsit.

The film was shot in Vancouver, Canada, Gregory Smith's hometown. Some fans of the book passed by the set and told the actors how much the book meant to them. "One woman came up crying and said that it touched her,"[3] Smith told Angelique Flores of *Video Store Magazine*.

After its showing on ABC, the movie was released on DVD. Smith did some interviews for the behind-the-scenes feature. He admitted that he is an avid collector of DVDs and owns 150 DVDs himself. He enjoys watching the behind-the-scenes features for movies, but he did not enjoy having to do it himself. "It's a neat experience as a fan to be a part of something else," he said of the extra features. Doing it himself, however, made him "self-conscious and afraid of saying something stupid or mispronouncing a word."[4]

Terry Kelleher, reporting for *People Weekly*, decided to watch the *Wrinkle* made-for-TV movie with a couple of 10-year olds, so she could get the feel of the target audience. One of the children noticed the differences between the movie and the book, but both children became wrapped up in the movie soon enough. Kelleher said that adults might consider the movie "overblown," but that they could be forgiving, because the message is positive. On the other hand, she thought that the movie got "preachy at the finish."[5]

L'Engle did not comment much about the movie version of *A Wrinkle in Time*. In a *Newsweek* interview, L'Engle admitted to having "glimpsed" the movie. She went on to say that she "expected it to be bad and it is."[6] Despite the author's criticisms, her official Web site lists fans' reviews of the film, which range from joy to disappointment. Many fans agreed with L'Engle that the movie did not live up to the book. Some thought that the movie they had created in their heads as they read was much better. Some felt that the special effects used to show tessering and IT were poorly done. Other fans thought the movie was accurate and very well done, but these fans were a minority: Most people were disappointed.

Wrinkle was also developed as a play. In 2004, Prime Stage Theater presented the story as part of the SciTech Festival in Pittsburgh, Pennsylvania. It was performed at the conclusion of the festival and was put on in the Carnegie Science Center. For this production, the artistic director of Prime Stage worked with playwright Brian Wongchaowart to adapt the book. They developed two scripts. One took place in over 90 minutes. The other, for matinee audiences, took place in 45 minutes.

In 2002, *The Arm of the Starfish* was made into a television movie. This movie stars Mischa Barton as Vicky, an actress best known for her role as Marissa Cooper on the television series *The O.C.* James Whitmore plays her dying grandfather, Ryan Merriman portrays Adam, and Jared Padalecki appears as Zachary. The movie was filmed in Australia and was broadcast on the Disney Channel on August 23, 2002.

The plot of *The Arm of the Starfish* film was vastly different from the book. In the movie, Vicky's parents hardly appear and the summer with the grandfather begins as a normal summer. The movie does not tell that he is dying until later on. The characters Leon and John are both missing from this version. The movie also contains an unlikely pairing between Adam and Zach. They team up to save dolphins from illegal drift nets.

Madeleine L'Engle at her desk in the library of the Cathedral of St. John the Divine in New York City, where she volunteered. The Cathedral is claimed to be the largest Anglican and fourth-largest Christian church in the world.

7

Tripping over Ideas

A ROOM OF HER OWN

By 1961, the Franklins wanted to move back to the city. They found an apartment in New York, and Hugh Franklin returned to his work in the theater. The children were sent to private schools in the city, and L'Engle returned to writing. A year later, *A Wrinkle in Time* was published. With her new work winning several awards in 1963, L'Engle became a literary star overnight, but it was just the beginning of her writing career. During the family's years of living full time in Connecticut, L'Engle worked out of Crosswicks while caring for the children and watching the store. The old house they bought was slowly renovated, and her office was the last room to be fixed because it was not a priority.

The room that became her office was a space above the garage that had been used by the previous owners as a chicken coop. When the Franklins bought the house and moved in, the floor was still covered with hay and chicken droppings! As it turned out, the droppings were great for the garden. They shoveled them out of the window for her husband to use as plant fertilizer. Fifteen years after they moved into the house, they were finally able to turn it into a comfortable working space for L'Engle. Her mother helped plan the office. Once it was finished, L'Engle declared the area private. No one was allowed in unless invited. Her children took to calling it the "Ivory Tower." Over the years, it became less private, as she allowed her children and their husbands to use it as a study while they were living at Crosswicks in the summers.

While the family lived in New York, L'Engle worked out of their apartment, until the distractions became too much to handle. One day, L'Engle wandered into the cathedral at St. John the Divine, where she went to church. She was looking for a quiet space in which to write. The librarian was preparing to leave on jury duty. L'Engle saw his typewriter and offered to take his place if she could use it. He agreed. The librarian did not return within a few days, and L'Engle became the volunteer librarian. She continued to use the office at the cathedral to do her work for many years.

MANUAL LABOR

Even if L'Engle had never had any of her work published, she would still be a writer. "It's very nice to be published," she admitted. "But being a writer means writing. . . . It means writing every day."[1] L'Engle compared what unpublished writers do to the work of the famous painter Vincent van Gogh, who sold just one painting in his lifetime. His brother bought it. Van Gogh was still a painter even though he did not have financial success or recognition during his lifetime. Similarly, L'Engle believed anyone who writes is a writer, regardless of whether they are published or not.

Many people think that writing is not real work, but L'Engle believed writing to be very hard work indeed. She thought of it as she did tuning an instrument or doing scales. If writers don't practice their art by writing every day, they lose the ability to write well.

Before the children were in school, finding time to write was a problem, so she made sure to work at night after they went to bed. This, she believed, is the writer's job. It needs to be done every day, and it needs to be done alone. Distractions can be deadly for stories, so writers need to schedule their writing time. They also need to make sure that they have a solitary place to work so that they can do so without any distractions. L'Engle always put in an eight-hour workday. "I do not work steadily nine to five. Nobody can. Your bottom would get sore."[2] She preferred to work early in the morning. Ideas were fresher and more creative for her in the morning hours. She also made sure to take breaks from her work. She walked the dogs while she was in Manhattan. At Crosswicks, she escaped to a nearby brook—far enough from the house that she could not hear someone if they called. L'Engle admitted to even writing while on vacation with her family. The only place she did not write was onboard a ship at night. When the lights were out, she liked to just stop and enjoy the darkness. If there was a movie playing, even a bad one, she took time out to watch.

L'Engle did not believe in using recording devices when she worked. She believed that writing is manual labor, to be done with the hands. Writing longhand or tapping the keys on a typewriter or computer is essential to the act of writing.

DON'T TRIP

After she became a popular author, L'Engle received more than 100 letters each week. In these letters, from both children and adults, she was often asked where she got her ideas. In response, she liked to tell a story about the composer Johann Sebastian Bach. In an interview for *Booklist,* she remarked, "When [Bach] was an old man, a young student said, 'Papa Bach, where did you get the ideas for all these melodies?' And the old man said, 'Why, when I get up in the morning, it's all I can do not to trip over them.' "[3] Bach worked for L'Engle in other ways too. When she suffered from writer's block, she would turn to Bach's music, playing the piano for about an hour. While she concentrated on the piano, her mind figured out what she needed to do next with her writing.

Of course, it's not enough to have the ideas. A writer has to make those ideas into a work that communicates with the reader. Learning from what her fans told her they created when they read her books, L'Engle believed that the reader is a co-creator of a book with the author. Once a fan asked L'Engle about the illustrations in one of her novels, although there were no illustrations. The reader had created images so vivid that he thought he was really seeing drawn pictures!

Despite the hard work and the loyalty of fans, L'Engle received her share of criticism and rejection. Even for a writer of her ability and success, rejection can be difficult.

In the many years that her work was being rejected, every rejection letter made her feel awful. She felt like they were rejecting her as a person, not just her work. She often said that she never wanted to feel that kind of rejection again. During that time, she put up a cartoon on her workroom wall. In it, a writer is shown leaving a publisher's office. His manuscript had just been rejected, so he is sad. "The caption says, 'We're very sorry, Mr. Tolstoy, but we aren't in the market for a war story right now.'"[4] L'Engle said that the cartoon had gotten her through some very hard times. Tolstoy is the author of the novel *War and Peace*, one of the most famous works of literature in history and considered by many to be the greatest novel of all time. Although *War and Peace* was not really rejected, the cartoon made L'Engle understand that even the best writers can be criticized.

Throughout her career, L'Engle tried to brush off praise as much as criticism. She did not like to pay attention to praise because she felt it distracted her from doing her best work. She believed that writers needed to throw themselves into their work—and ignore everything else.

Did you know...

Because of L'Engle's vast body of work, she created a business to handle all her intellectual property. Run by her family, Crosswicks, Ltd. holds the copyright for all of L'Engle's work. The official location of Crosswicks, Ltd. is the Cathedral Library at St. John the Divine in New York.

So why write? After all the rejections and uncertainty of her early years, L'Engle never gave up the idea of becoming a writer. She said that she was compelled to keep writing. But why? At a lecture one summer, L'Engle stated, "The artist's response to the irrationality of the world is to paint or sing or write."[5] What she meant was that the world is unpredictable. Artists, like writers, try to find balance in this unpredictable world by creating a world that they can control. As for writing a good book, L'Engle did not worry about that either. She tried to remember that, as a writer, her job was simply to write as good a book as she could while she was working. That is a writer's only job.

THE DELIGHTS OF WRITING

As a famous children's book author, L'Engle was invited to lecture all over the world. She taught classes as a visiting professor at colleges, and sometimes she taught creative writing classes at the private school in Manhattan where her children attended. Even though she taught those creative writing classes, L'Engle did not believe that creativity could be taught. She did, however, believe that a person's creativity could be destroyed if not given the opportunity to grow. When she taught, she preferred calling the exercises "writing practices" instead of "creative writing." She said that writing practice is like finger exercises on a piano. To learn to write well, a student needs to read great writers, such as Tolstoy. After reading several of the great pieces of literature, readers learn that there are certain things that the best writers always do and certain things that they never do. This, she believed, is the best kind of writing instruction. What L'Engle demonstrated to budding writers in her classes were the tools of writing. One of the most important tools is punctuation. L'Engle admitted to breaking punctuation rules in her writing, but she told all her students that they must know what the rules are before they break them, and that they must have a good reason for breaking them.

She also shared some writing rules with her students. At the beginning of every story, she noted that "a writer should immediately tell the reader four things:

1. Who the story is about.
2. What he is doing.
3. Where he is doing it.
4. When he is doing it."[6]

Throughout the story, it is the job of the writer to show what is happening. To do this, the writer must use the senses—touch, smell, taste, hearing, and sight—to describe the characters and setting. For L'Engle, there is also another sense in her writing: a moral one. In literature, there is a structure. The plot of a story provides structure. In every story, there must be a beginning, middle, and end, and there must be a problem and a solution. However, L'Engle taught that writers are free to do whatever they like, even within a strict structure. In *A Wrinkle in Time,* Mrs Whatsit tries to explain this to Calvin. She uses the example of iambic pentameter, which is a structure that is used to write sonnets, a form of poetry:

"There are fourteen lines, I believe, all in iambic pentameter. That's a very strict rhythm or meter, yes?"

"Yes," Calvin nodded.

"And each line has to end with a precise rhyme pattern. And if the poet does not do it exactly this way, it is not a sonnet, is it?"

"No."

"But within this strict form the poet has complete freedom to say whatever he wants, doesn't he?"[7]

To work in a structure, a writer needs to find the right words to tell the story. As a young girl, L'Engle learned new words by reading them in the books that her teacher, Miss Clapp, assigned to her. She never used a dictionary to look up words she did not understand. She just continued reading, and the meaning would become clear after she had seen the word a few times in different places. L'Engle liked to quote a poem written by an anonymous poet many years ago:

> The written word
>
> Should be clean as bone,
>
> Clear as light,
>
> Firm as stone.
>
> Two words are not
>
> As good as one.[8]

L'Engle believed writers should be free to use any words to communicate their stories, even if they believe such words might be unfamiliar to the reader. She believed that the reader would grow as a reader by learning new words. It upset her that some vocabulary that was used a long time ago is now lost forever. She wished that modern writers would read sixteenth and seventeenth century poetry and incorporate the vocabulary of that time into their work so that those words would come back to life.

She also believed that writers need to listen to their stories. She remarked, "You listen and you say 'a ha,' and you write it down. A lot of it is not planned, not conscious; it happens while you're doing it."[9] The unplanned parts of L'Engle's stories often happened when the characters took over. She would say that her characters pushed her and pulled her and went places she did not want them to go. "They tell me. I'm not in charge," she said. "I'm not a dictator. I listen to them."[10] When L'Engle was writing *The Arm of the Starfish,* she said that the character Joshua Archer simply appeared in the book. She had not planned for that character at all. She was surprised to find him in her story, and she had to rewrite about half the book to make the story fit his surprise entrance. She believed that one of the greatest pleasures of writing is being surprised to find words that the writer never expected to write appear on the page.

Although some characters might have surprised L'Engle when they appeared in her stories, they were often based on the people in her life or on L'Engle herself. Her family was sometimes at odds with her over the characters in her books, even her nonfiction. They think that her nonfiction is more made-up than her stories. One of her sons-in-law once said that L'Engle considered everything in her journal to be the absolute truth. He said that this was "a hilarious statement." Her journals were anything but absolute truth. Her adopted daughter, Maria, called her autobiography *Two-Part Invention* "a lovely fairy tale." The family felt that her fiction, on the other hand, was very autobiographical. Some felt that their lives and likenesses were used too freely in her novels.

A photo of Madeleine L'Engle and Hugh Franklin. Franklin often inspired L'Engle's work, including a vivid passage in her journals in which he, as a member of the volunteer fire department, dashed out in the middle of the night to keep the Brechstein family's house from burning down—a family and incident she completely invented!

The setting for both *Meet the Austins* and *A Wrinkle in Time* was Crosswicks. The characters Meg and Vicky are based on L'Engle herself. The child prodigies, Rob Austin and Charles Wallace, are based on L'Engle's son, Bion. The adopted child in *Meet the Austins* is, of course, her daughter

Maria. Now a photographer, Maria collaborated with L'Engle on a photo book about mothers and daughters. As she grew older, Maria said that she was no longer upset about her appearances in L'Engle's work or the inaccuracies in her mother's nonfiction: "She's such a storyteller that she gets confused about what really happened."[11]

L'Engle's journals were an important tool in her writing. She used them to respond to the events in her life and referred back to them to remind herself of past events. In the first of the Crosswicks Journals, *A Circle of Quiet,* L'Engle tells a story about a family called the Brechsteins, who moved to Goshen, Connecticut. They lived near the Crosswicks house while L'Engle and Franklin lived there year-round. She describes the family in detail, the wife and husband and their three boys. She even goes on to describe a part of their house burning down. Her husband, as part of the volunteer fire department, had to run out in the middle of the night to help subdue the fire. L'Engle herself and the other wives in town called each other on the phone with information and eventually went to the house with food for the family. L'Engle does not mention until several pages later that she invented the Brechstein family. None of what she described in that part of her autobiography actually happened. She admitted this freely to her readers, but only her family would know for sure what else she made up in her nonfiction work.

WRITING FOR CHILDREN

As a writer of fiction, nonfiction, and religious books, L'Engle is almost impossible to categorize as a writer. She also detested labels. "I'm not a children's writer," she once said. "I'm not a Christian writer. I resist and reject that kind of classification. I'm a writer period. People underestimate children. They think you have to write differently. You don't. You just have to tell a story."[12] She was horrified when she learned that one of the best writers of books for teens announced that he was not going to write for that age group any longer. He said it was because his children had grown up and he did not understand kids anymore. L'Engle believed that the basic truths about people never changes, and that writers should write the same for children as they do for adults. The literary rules that apply to *The Brothers Karamazov,* a well-respected adult novel by Fyodor Dostoevsky, should also apply to *Peter Rabbit* by Beatrix Potter, a children's book classic. She once wrote that the idea that "you write for children only when you can't make it in the real world, because writing for children is easier [is] wrong, wrong, wrong!"[13] If a book is not good enough for *everyone* to read, she believed, it certainly is not good enough for children.

L'Engle opposed some of the language that is used in children's books today. She felt that the violence and sexual content is misplaced and harmful. She also disliked the use of curse words simply for shock value. For her, it took away the value of the words when they are used all over the place. While she was against censorship, she believed that both writers and publishers ought to look at literature with more substance, rather than simply sensational stories.

What were among L'Engle's favorite books for children? *The Secret Garden* by Frances Hodgson Burnett, *Lord of the Flies* by William Golding, and *The Lord of the Rings* by J.R.R. Tolkien are three she held up as examples of excellent and lasting children's fiction. As for more modern children's literature, L'Engle was not as keen on the popular books. She found the Harry Potter series to be good entertainment, but felt there was nothing beneath it—no moral undercurrent to the story.

THE WRITING LIFE

Although she liked writing in her office, L'Engle sometimes found writing away from home to be beneficial. In an interview with Carole F. Chase, she said,

> I find airports and planes and hotel rooms excellent places in which to write, because while I am in them, I am not responsible for anything except my work. . . . In a hotel room I do not have to think about the vacuum cleaner (though sometimes I would like to have one); domestic chores are not my responsibility; I am free to write.[14]

She often likened writing to cooking—on her stove several big pots would be going at the same time. A scene went in one pot and a character in another. Sometimes she found things that she had not realized she had added. Then she would arrange or rearrange everything until she found her story.

A photo of Madeleine L'Engle at her desk. Poor health slowed her creative output in her later years.

8

Her Story

L'ENGLE'S OWN LIFE was as interesting and filled with adventure and exotic people and locations as any character she wrote about. L'Engle's upbringing was certainly different. How many American children are brought up by English nannies? How many move to Europe and attend boarding schools in Switzerland? When L'Engle moved out on her own in her early twenties, the adventures continued. She was an actress who married a fellow actor and became a published novelist. Then she and her husband both put their careers on hold to move to a farm in Connecticut and raise their children. When the two returned to New York and their respective careers resumed, they seemed to work harder and better than ever. The decade-long hiatus in Connecticut did nothing to dull their talent.

ACCOLADES

L'Engle won many prestigious awards throughout her career for her body of work. Her first—and one of her most notable awards—came when *A Wrinkle in Time* won the John Newbery Medal in 1963. Another important honor came to her in 1984 when her alma mater, Smith College, honored her with the Sophia Award for distinction in her field. In 1986, the National Council of Teachers of English awarded her the ALAN (Assembly on Literature for Adolescents) Award for Outstanding Contribution to Adolescent Literature.

In 1997, the World Fantasy Convention presented her with a lifetime achievement award. According to the official Web site, this award has been given out since 1975 to "recognize outstanding work in the fantasy genre."[1] The award ceremonies take place all over the world. The year L'Engle was recognized, the convention was held in England. The following year, she was given the Margaret A. Edwards Award. Established in 1988, the award honors an author's lifetime achievement for writing a body of work that is popular with teens. Specifically, "it recognizes an author's work in helping adolescents become aware of themselves and addressing questions about their role and importance in relationships, society, and in the world."[2] It is given out by YALSA (Young Adult Library Services Association) and sponsored by *School Library Journal.*

On Wednesday, November 17, 2004, just shy of her 86th birthday, L'Engle was honored with the National Humanities Medal. According to the National Endowment of the

Arts Web site, "The National Humanities Medal, inaugurated in 1997, honors individuals or groups whose work has deepened the nation's understanding of the humanities, broadened our citizens' engagement with the humanities, or helped preserve and expand Americans' access to important resources in the humanities."[3] At the time the award was given, L'Engle was in the hospital, recuperating from a fall. Her granddaughter, Charlotte Jones, traveled to Washington, D.C., to accept the award on her behalf at the White House.

L'Engle was given more than a dozen honorary degrees. An honorary degree is given by colleges to a person as recognition of their work, not for completing the school's coursework. Some of L'Engle's honorary degrees are from theological schools. The honorary Doctor of Sacred Theology was given to her in 1984 from Berkeley Divinity School, in California. The honorary Doctor of Humane Letters was awarded to her the year before from the Christian Theological Seminary in Indianapolis.

FAITH AND ADVERSITY

Although some Christians value L'Engle's work as faithful and spiritual, others question her motives and find her work anti-Christian. Oddly, the work that receives the most anti-Christian sentiment is *A Wrinkle in Time*. When *Wrinkle* was listed among the 10 most banned books, L'Engle said she felt honored because she was listed alongside other great writers like Mark Twain, who wrote *The Adventures of Huckleberry Finn* and *The Adventures of Tom Sawyer*, and John Steinbeck, the Pulitzer prize-winning author of *The Grapes of Wrath*. Steinbeck also won a Nobel Prize for Literature in his lifetime—one of the most prestigious awards given to writers.

One day in 1986, Franklin was home ill. He was reading the newspaper and handed it to L'Engle so she could read an article about parents in Tennessee who were trying to ban textbooks because they might cause kids to use their imaginations. At the time, L'Engle was still smarting from the blows of attackers who objected to the themes in *A Wrinkle in Time.* She thought the people who objected to her work were "mildly insane." Her husband figured that those people were afraid. L'Engle did not know how to exist without imagination. She also felt that believing in a God who can create all things "takes all the imagination with which we have been endowed."[4]

L'Engle's work tried to answer the question: "Who am I?" She took the Bible as truth but not necessarily fact. The reason she gave for this opinion was that she took the Bible too seriously to view it as a literal text. By this, she meant that facts are things that can be proven. However, something can be true without it being a provable fact. In her Margaret A. Edwards Award acceptance speech, L'Engle noted that "truth and fact are not the same thing. Truth does not contradict or deny facts, but it goes through and beyond facts."[5] For instance, you can prove what color your hair is

Did you know...

L'Engle is one of the Christian authors listed on the Web site www.passageway.org. This is a site for teens run by the Billy Graham Evangelistic Association. She is featured along with J.R.R. Tolkien (*The Lord of the Rings*) and C.S. Lewis (*The Chronicles of Narnia*).

by looking at your hair. You cannot prove the amount of someone's love, even if you can feel that love. She said that when she was writing *A Wrinkle in Time,* "I was looking for truth,"[6] not fact.

A writer for Watchman Fellowship did not agree with L'Engle's views. *The Watchman Expositor* published an article saying that her views did not hold up to the Bible. Not only did she admit that she did not view the Bible as fact, the author of the article claimed that "her view also ignores the holiness and wrath of a just God."[7] L'Engle, however, did not believe in a God that punishes people.

For L'Engle, science and religion were not mutually exclusive. In an interview, she noted,

> All science can do is open up a wider understanding of the universe. I mean, God doesn't change, we change in what we believe. And because we no longer think we're a little planet with everything whirling around us—the center of the universe—our idea of God has changed along with that.[8]

L'Engle was referring to a time when many people believed that the Earth was the center of the universe. When Galileo Galilei, an Italian astronomer, proved that the Earth revolved around the sun and not the other way around, people were shocked. Some people called him a heretic, or someone whose views do not agree with their church. However, now people know that the Earth does in fact move around the sun, and that does not change anything other than their knowledge of science.

HEALTH AND FAMILY

L'Engle's father and mother suffered serious health issues, and L'Engle herself was not immune to physical challenges. In addition to needing to wear false teeth and having an illness make one leg shorter than the other, in fourth grade, she suffered from a disease called iritis. The disease causes an inflammation in the iris of the eyes and can possibly cause blindness. L'Engle was told that, if the inflammation ever happened again, she could go blind. In later years, when she did suffer from iritis again, the pain became almost unbearable. A friend asked if she thought it would be better to be blind rather than suffer through all the pain. L'Engle was adamant that being blind would certainly not be better. She was ordered not to read at all, but she took a risk and read and wrote in her journal a little.

In the summer of 1968, L'Engle's first granddaughter was born. She was also named Madeleine, but nicknamed Lena. The following year, another granddaughter, Charlotte, was born. Both were Josephine's daughters. In the summer of 1971, when L'Engle's mother came to stay at Crosswicks, she was very ill. The family hired a few helpers to take care of her. That summer, there were three Madeleines in the house, but it was not to last.

L'Engle and her husband knew that her mother could not make the trip back to her home in Jacksonville, Florida. They began to think about what they would do at the end of the summer. L'Engle needed to return to St. John the Divine to reopen the library, and Franklin needed to return to work. The women who were taking care of L'Engle's mother that summer would be returning to college in September. Unfortunately, the resolution to their problem came quickly and unpleasantly. L'Engle and Franklin left Crosswicks to drive to New York to attend the wedding of a friend. They left L'Engle's mother, Bion and his wife, L'Engle's granddaughters, and the girls who cared for her mother. It was to be a short trip of only 24 hours. L'Engle felt that everything would be all right. When she and her husband arrived in the city, she called home to check on things. Bion answered the phone. He said, "Grandmother died, about four this afternoon."[9] L'Engle regretted she was on the highway driving to Manhattan when her mother passed away. She wrote about that last summer with her mother in *The Summer of the Great-Grandmother* (1974).

L'Engle moved back to New York as planned at the end of the summer, and the following summer, she had the odd experience of absorbing her mother's belongings into her household. Luckily, there were many other distractions. Other grandchildren had arrived. In 1977, Josephine had a son named Edward. In 1985, Maria had her first child, Bryson.

Early in 1986, L'Engle and Franklin traveled to the Virgin Islands on vacation. L'Engle was scheduled to lecture in China, but she was ill and could not go alone, so her husband accompanied her. When they returned, Maria had another baby, whom they named Alexander. L'Engle, however, barely had time to enjoy her new grandson. Franklin fell ill and visited his doctor for a small problem. The doctor decided to do a few tests, and detected cancer. It was quite a blow for the family.

Franklin's health quickly worsened. He spent most of the summer in the hospital, undergoing treatment. He spent his seventieth birthday in a hospital bed, instead of on the trip the family had been planning for him. When he fell ill, they decided to have a dinner instead, thinking that his illness would have left him by then. He and their granddaughter, Charlotte, were used to spending their birthdays together, because they were only two days apart. That year, the tradition they had for 17 years was broken.

Franklin endured a series of operations and procedures at the hospital, and L'Engle spent more than seven hours a day there with him. She had a small electric typewriter with her at times but found working extremely difficult. When Franklin finally died in the hospital, L'Engle was with him, holding him. Two years later, *Two-Part Invention* was published. It tells the story of L'Engle and Franklin's marriage and the emotional turmoil surrounding his sudden death.

L'Engle managed to go on, caring for her family and writing books. In 1991, during a trip to San Diego, she was involved in an automobile accident. She was severely injured but recovered well. The following year, L'Engle visited Antarctica with her son, Bion, and his wife, Laurie. She used the scenery of that trip as the setting for the next Austin book, *Troubling a Star* (1994).

L'Engle continued to suffer injuries as she maintained her schedule of lectures, and they began to slow her down. In 1996, she underwent foot and ankle surgery. In 1999, after her first great-grandchild was born, she broke her hip. Later that year, Bion, who had been suffering from liver problems, died.

L'Engle's first picture book, *The Other Dog* was published in 2001. It was about Touché, who resents the new dog that has come into the family. What Touché does not realize is that the new dog is a baby. A reviewer for *Publisher's Weekly* called it an "impish, tongue-in-cheek memoir."[10]

On February 3, 2002, L'Engle suffered a stroke. Her recovery went well. In 2003, she was given a pacemaker for her heart. Her various illnesses had slowed her down considerably. L'Engle's humor and cheerfulness, however, helped her achieve many of her goals as an artist. Until the end of her life, she was still writing, still talking, and still asking the big questions about life and the universe. If anything, she felt freer in her later years. In a 2004 interview, she said that because she was older she didn't mince words. "I can say what I want, and I don't get punished for it."[11]

Madeleine L'Engle died on September 6, 2007, leaving behind an immense and remarkable body of work that will be treasured by longtime fans—and new ones—for years to come.

CHRONOLOGY

1918 On November 29, Madeleine L'Engle Camp is born in New York City.

1923 She writes her first story at age five.

1930 The Camp family moves to Europe.

1931 The family returns to the United States; she enrolls at Ashley Hall.

1935 L'Engle's father dies.

1936 L'Engle enters Smith College in Northampton, Massachusetts.

1941 L'Engle graduates from Smith with honors in English; she moves to Greenwich Village in New York City and pursues a writing career.

1943 L'Engle acts in the play *The Cherry Orchard*; she meets fellow actor Hugh Franklin.

1944 She begins to write under the name L'Engle.

1945 Vanguard Press publishes her first novel, *The Small Rain*.

1946 L'Engle and Franklin are married on January 26; they purchase Crosswicks.

1947 Josephine Franklin is born.

1952 The family moves to Crosswicks full time; Hugh Franklin temporarily gives up his acting career; they buy and run a general store; Bion Franklin is born.

1957 The Franklins adopt seven-year-old Maria.

1959 L'Engle begins to write *A Wrinkle in Time*.

1960 The Franklins sell the store and move back to New York City.

1962 *A Wrinkle in Time* is published by Farrar, Straus.

1963 *A Wrinkle in Time* wins the Newbery Medal.

1965 L'Engle becomes writer-in-residence at the Cathedral of St. John the Divine.

1981 Smith College awards the Smith Medal to L'Engle.

1986 Hugh Franklin dies.

1997 L'Engle receives a World Fantasy Award for lifetime achievement from the World Fantasy Convention.

1998 L'Engle receives the Margaret A. Edwards Award for lifetime achievement.

1999 Bion Franklin dies; L'Engle's first great-grandchild is born.

2001 Her last new work, *The Other Dog*, is published; miniseries version of *A Wrinkle in Time* appears on Australian and German television.

2002 L'Engle suffers a stroke.

2003 L'Engle is outfitted with a pacemaker for her heart.

2004 L'Engle is awarded the National Humanities Medal on November 17; the re-edited and re-shot version of *A Wrinkle in Time* is shown on ABC.

2007 Madeleine L'Engle dies on September 6.

NOTES

Chapter 1

1 Cynthia Zarin, "The Storyteller; Profiles," *New Yorker* (2004): p. 60.

2 Madeleine L'Engle, *The Summer of the Great-Grandmother*. New York: Farrar, Straus & Giroux, 1974, p. 4.

3 Zarin, "The Storyteller; Profiles," p. 60.

4 "Author Spotlight: Madeleine L'Engle." Random House Web site. http://www.randomhouse.com/author/results.pperl?authorid=16446.

5 Madeleine L'Engle, *Madeleine L'Engle Herself: Reflections on a Writing Life*. Compiled by Carole F. Chase. Colorado Springs, Colo.: Waterbrook Press, 2001, p. 70.

6 Ibid.

7 Donald R. Gallo, *Speaking for Ourselves*. Urban, Ill.: National Council of Teachers of English, 1990, p. 116.

8 L'Engle, *Madeleine L'Engle Herself*, p. 25.

9 "Ashley Hall Home Page." Ashley Hall Web site. http://www.ashleyhall.org.

10 "Madeleine L'Engle." Ashley Hall Web site. http://www.ashleyhall.org.

11 "Home Page." Smith College Web site. http://www.smith.edu.

Chapter 2

1 Zarin, "The Storyteller; Profiles," p. 60.

2 Madeleine L'Engle, *Two-Part Invention: The Story of a Marriage*. New York: Farrar, Straus & Giroux, 1988, p. 25.

3 Ibid., p. 44.

4 Ibid., p. 45.

5 Ibid., p. 130.

Chapter 3

1 Madeleine L'Engle, *A Circle of Quiet*. New York: Farrar, Straus & Giroux, 1972, p. 19.

2 "Author Spotlight: Madeleine L'Engle," Waterbrook Press Web site. http://www.randomhouse.com/author/results.pperl?authorid=16446.

3 Sally Estes, "The Booklist Interview: Madeleine L'Engle," *Booklist* (1998): pp. 16–20.

4 Susan Kruglinski, "20 Things You Didn't Know About . . . Relativity." *Discover*, February 25, 2008. http://discovermagazine.com/2008/mar/20-things-you-didn.t-know-about-relativity/?searchterm=theory%20of%20relativity.

5 "Spotlight on…Madeleine L'Engle." Teachers @ Random Web site. http://www.randomhouse.

com/teachers/authors/results.
pperl?authorid=16446.

6 L'Engle, *Madeleine L'Engle Herself*, p. 75.

7 "Author Spotlight: Madeleine L'Engle." Waterbrook Press Web site. http://www.randomhouse.com/author/results.pperl?authorid=16446

8 L'Engle, *Madeleine L'Engle Herself*, p. 75.

9 L'Engle, *A Circle of Quiet*, p. 217.

10 Madeleine L'Engle, "Newbery Acceptance Speech." Madeleine L'Engle Web site. http://www.madeleinelengle.com/reference/newberyspeech.htm.

11 Barbara L. Talcroft, "Review of *A Wrinkle in Time*."' Barnes and Noble Web site, Children's Literature. http://search.barnesandnoble.com/Wrinkle-in-Time/Madeleine-LEngle/e/9780312367541/?itm=1.

12 Estes, "The Booklist Interview: Madeleine L'Engle," pp. 16–20.

13 L'Engle, *A Circle of Quiet*, pp. 138–139.

Chapter 4

1 Madeleine L'Engle, *A Wrinkle in Time*. New York: Farrar, Straus & Giroux, 1962, p. 150.

2 Lisa Sonne, "A Stardust Journey with *A Wrinkle in Time*," introduction to *A Wrinkle in Time*, by Madeleine L'Engle. New York: Farrar, Straus & Giroux, 1962, p. iii.

3 Suzanne Macneille, "Coming of Age: Mostly a Matter of Time," *New York Times*, May 19, 2004, pp. 13–14.

4 L'Engle, *A Circle of Quiet*, p. 89.

5 Robert Hatch and William Hatch, *The Hero Project*. New York: McGraw Hill, 2006, p. 29.

6 Zarin, "The Storyteller; Profiles," p. 60.

7 Hatch and Hatch, *The Hero Project*, p. 26.

8 John Rowe Townsend, *A Sense of Story: Essays on Contemporary Writers for Children*. London: Longman, 1971.

9 L'Engle, *A Circle of Quiet*, p. 137.

10 Barbara L. Talcroft, "Review of *A Wrinkle in Time*." *Children's Literature*, http://search.barnesandnoble.com/Wrinkle-in-Time/Madeleine-LEngle/e/9780312367541/?itm=1.

Chapter 5

1 L'Engle, *A Circle of Quiet*, p. 93.

2 "Review of *Troubling a Star*." *Publishers Weekly*, Amazon.com. http://www.amazon.com/Troubling-Star-Austin-Family-Chronicles/dp/031237934X/ref=pd_bbs_sr_1?ie=UTF8&s=books&qid=1226168799&sr=8-1.

3 Susan L. Rogers, "Review of *Troubling a Star*." *School Library Journal*, Amazon.com. http://www.amazon.com/Troubling-Star-Austin-Family-Chronicles/dp/031237934X/ref=pd_bbs_sr_1?ie=UTF8&s=books&qid=1226168799&sr=8-1.

4 "Definition of Kairos." All Words Web site. http://www.allwords.com/word-kairos.html.

5 "Review of *A Wind in the Door*." Amazon.com. http://www.amazon.

com/Wind-Door-MadeleineLEngle/dp/0312368542/ref=pd_bbs_sr_1?ie=UTF8&s=books&qid=1226168978&sr=8-1

6 Emilie Coulter, "Review of *A Swiftly Tilting Planet*." Amazon.com. http://www.amazon.com/Swiftly-Tilting-Planet-Madeleine-LEngle/dp/0312368569/ref=pd_bxgy_b_text_b.

7 Cindy Lombardo, "Review of *A Swiftly Tilting Planet*." *School Library Journal*, Amazon.com. http://www.amazon.ca/Swiftly-Tilting-Planet-Madeleine-LEngle/dp/0440901588.

8 Christine Behrman, "Review of *Many Waters*." *School Library Journal*, Amazon.com. http://www.amazon.com/Many-Waters-Time-Quartet-Bk/dp/0440405483.

9 "Review of *An Acceptable Time*." *VOYA*, Amazon.com. http://www.amazon.com/Acceptable-Time-Quartet-Bk/dp/product-description/0440208149.

10 "Description of *The Weather of the Heart*." Madeleine L'Engle Web site. http://www.madeleinelengle.com/books/weather.htm.

Chapter 6

1 "A 'Wrinkle' in Primetime," *School Library Journal* (2001): http://www.schoollibraryjournal.com/article/CA90697.html.

2 Nick Rafeal, "Wrinkle's a Fantastic Journey," *Boston Globe* (2004): p. 4.

3 Angelique Flores, "'Everwood' Star Gets into 'Wrinkle,'" *Video Store Magazine* (2004): p. 12.

4 Ibid.

5 Terry Kelleher, "A Wrinkle in Time: ABC review," *People Weekly* (2004): p. 38.

6 Melinda Henneberger, "I Dare You." *Newsweek* (2004): http://www.newsweek.com/id/105017.

Chapter 7

1 L'Engle, *Madeleine L'Engle Herself*, p. 34.

2 Ibid., p. 187.

3 Talcroft, "Review of *A Wrinkle in Time*." http://search.barnesandnoble.com/Wrinkle-in-Time/Madeleine-LEngle/e/9780312367541/?itm=1.

4 L'Engle, *Madeleine L'Engle Herself*, p. 106.

5 L'Engle, *The Summer of the Great-Grandmother*, p. 14.

6 L'Engle, *A Circle of Quiet*, p. 62.

7 L'Engle, *A Wrinkle in Time*, p. 186.

8 L'Engle, *A Circle of Quiet*, p. 149.

9 Shel Horowitz, "Madeleine L'Engle; Faith During Adversity." Frugal Fun Web site. http://www.frugalfun.com/l'engle.html.

10 Estes, "The Booklist Interview: Madeleine L'Engle," pp. 16–20.

11 Zarin, "The Storyteller; Profiles," p. 60.

12 Caroline Kim, "Telling Stories," *Humanities* (2005).

13 L'Engle, "Is It Good Enough for Children?," p. 8.

14 Carole F. Chase, "Words of Wisdom from Madeleine L'Engle," *Writer* (2002): p. 26.

Chapter 8

1 "1997 World Fantasy Award Winners and Nominees." World Fantasy Award Web site. http://www.worldfantasy.org/awards/1997.html.

2 "Margaret A. Edwards Award." American Library Association Web site. http://www.ala.org/ala/yalsa/booklistsawards/margaretaedwards/margaretedwards.htm.

3 "Who We Are." National Endowment for the Humanities Web site. http://www.neh.gov/whoweare/awards.html.

4 L'Engle, *Two-Part Invention: The Story of a Marriage*, p. 145.

5 Madeleine L'Engle, "Margaret A. Edwards Acceptance Speech." Madeleine L'Engle Web site. http://www.madeleinelengle.com/reference/libspeech.htm.

6 L'Engle, *A Circle of Quiet*, p. 149.

7 Craig Branch, "New Age Infiltrates American Life." *Watchman Fellowship*. http://www.geocities.com/Athens/Acropolis/8838/whine.html.

8 Karin Snelson, "A New Wrinkle: A Conversation with Madeleine L'Engle." Amazon.com. http://www.amazon.com/gp/feature.html?docId=6238.

9 L'Engle, *The Summer of the Great-Grandmother*, p. 227.

10 "Review of *The Other Dog*." *Publishers Weekly*, Amazon.com. http://www.amazon.com/Other-Dog-Madeleine-LEngle/dp/0811852288.

11 Kelleher, "A Wrinkle in Time: ABC Review," p. 38.

WORKS BY MADELEINE L'ENGLE

1944 *18 Washington Square South: A Comedy in One Act*

1945 *The Small Rain*

1946 *Ilsa*

1949 *And Both Were Young*

1951 *Camilla Dickinson*

1957 *A Winter's Love*

1960 *Meet the Austins*

1962 *A Wrinkle in Time*

1963 *The Moon by Night*

1964 *The Twenty-Four Days Before Christmas*

1965 *The Arm of the Starfish*; *Camilla* (revised)

1966 *The Love Letters*

1967 *The Journey with Jonah*

1968 *The Young Unicorns*

1969 *Dance in the Desert*; *Lines Scribbled on an Envelope and Other Poems*

1971 *The Other Side of the Sun*

1972 *A Circle of Quiet*

1973 *A Wind in the Door*

1974 *Everyday Prayers*; *Prayers for Sunday*; *The Risk of Birth*; *The Summer of the Great Grandmother*

1976 *Dragons in the Waters*

1977 *The Irrational Season*

1978 *The Weather of the Heart*; *A Swiftly Tilting Planet*

1979 *Ladders of Angels*

1980 *The Anti-Muffins*; *A Ring of Endless Light*; *Walking on Water: Reflections on Faith and Art*

1982 *A Severed Wasp*; *The Sphinx at Dawn*

1983 *And It Was Good: Reflections on Beginnings*

1984 *A House like a Lotus*

1985 *Trailing Clouds of Glory: Spiritual Values in Children's Literature* (with Avery Brooke)

1986 *A Stone for a Pillow: Journeys with Jacob*; *Many Waters*

1987 *A Cry like a Bell*

1988 *Reading Together* (audio tape of L'Engle and Franklin); *Two-Part Invention*

1989 *Sold into Egypt: Joseph's Journey into Human Being*; *An Acceptable Time*

1990 *The Glorious Impossible*

1992 *Certain Women*

1993 *The Rock that Is Higher*

1994 *Troubling a Star*; *Anytime Prayers*

1996 *Glimpses of Grace* (with Carole Chase); *Penguins and Golden Calves: Icons and Idols*; *A Live Coal in the Sea*; *Wintersong* (with Luci Shaw)

1997 *Mothers and Daughters* (with Maria Rooney); *Bright Evening Star*; *Friends for the Journey* (with Luci Shaw)

1999 *Mothers and Sons* (with Maria Rooney); *Prayerbook for Spiritual Friends* (with Luci Shaw); *A Full House*

2001 *The Other Dog*; *Madeleine L'Engle Herself: Reflections on a Writing Life* (with Carole Chase)

2005 *The Ordering of Love: The New and Collected Poems of Madeleine L'Engle*

2008 *The Joys of Love*

POPULAR BOOKS

THE ARM OF THE STARFISH

Adam Eddington is a marine biology student studying in Portugal. He finds himself caught between the attentions of two girls—Kali Cutter, who he meets at the airport on his way to Portugal—and Poly O'Keefe, the daughter of the scientist he is studying with. He also finds himself in a deeper conflict that could affect the entire world. Adam must decide which side he is on.

MANY WATERS

The third book in the "Time Fantasy" series deals with Meg's twin brothers, Sandy and Dennys Murry. They are accidentally sent back to biblical times. They find themselves in a hot desert, where mythical animals appear. There is a man named Noah who is building a boat to prepare for a great flood.

MEET THE AUSTINS

This is the first book in the "Austin Family" series. Vicky Austin is the second child and oldest daughter of the four Austin kids. All their lives are changed when the family adopts seven-year old Maggy Hamilton, who is orphaned by the sudden death of her father. The siblings struggle to accept Maggy who makes their lives difficult.

A RING OF ENDLESS LIGHT

Vicky Austin and her family are spending the summer with her grandfather. He is dying of cancer. She finds herself embroiled in relationships with three very different boys. Zachary is attractive, but troubled. His attempted suicide causes Commander Rodney's death. Leo, the commander's son, wants her comfort. Adam, her older brother's friend allows her to help with his experiments on dolphins, but treats her like a little girl, when she wants him to see her as grown-up.

A SWIFTLY TILTING PLANET

Charles Wallace meets a unicorn named Gaudior and journeys through time to stop a dictator called Maddog Branzillo. His actions threaten the future of the world. Charles Wallace works through the bodies of four people from different time periods to try to stop the tragic chain of events that the dictator sets off.

A WIND IN THE DOOR

The second book in the "Time Fantasy" series finds Meg and Charles Wallace in a struggle between life and death. Charles Wallace sees dragons in the vegetable garden. The dragons warn the children of danger ahead, and Meg and Calvin once again travel into space to save Charles Wallace from evil.

A WRINKLE IN TIME

Meg Murry, her brother, Charles Wallace, and schoolmate, Calvin O'Keefe, travel through a tesseract—a wrinkle in time—to rescue her father from a planet called Camazotz and an evil brain called IT, which threatens the entire universe and everyone in it to a life of conformity. Extraterrestrial beings help them along the way. This is the first work of fantasy and science fiction with a female hero.

POPULAR CHARACTERS

CALVIN O'KEEFE

Calvin first appears in *A Wrinkle in Time* as Meg's friend. He is socially well adjusted, a good sport, and a good student. He also has some psychic abilities that are revealed in this first novel. Later, he marries Meg Murry and becomes a marine biologist.

CHARLES WALLACE MURRY

The youngest Murry child, Charles Wallace is extraordinarily intelligent. His mitochondria provide the setting for *A Wind in the Door.* He is small for his age, and his intelligence and quietness are misunderstood by his peers. He is bullied as a child.

MARGARET "MEG" MURRY

Meg is the protagonist of the "Time Fantasy" series, beginning with *A Wrinkle in Time.* As a young woman, she is somewhat awkward and plain, and feels like an outsider. She is closest to her youngest brother, Charles Wallace. As an adult, she marries Calvin O'Keefe. They have seven children. She is a mathematical genius.

ROB AUSTIN

Rob, the youngest of the Austin children, is curious and insightful. He is based on L'Engle's son, Bion.

VICKY AUSTIN

Vicky is the heroine of the "Austin Family" series. Vicky is a poet and writer. She has psychic abilities that are revealed in *The Arm of the Starfish.* Vicky is usually the narrator in the Austin series of books.

MAJOR AWARDS

1963 *A Wrinkle in Time* wins the John Newbery Medal.

1964 *A Wrinkle in Time* is runner up for the Hans Christian Anderson Award.

1965 *A Wrinkle in Time* wins the Sequoyah Award and the Lewis Carroll Shelf Award.

1969 *The Moon by Night* wins the Austrian State Literary Prize.

1971 *Camilla* wins the Austrian State Literary Prize.

1980 *A Ring of Endless Light* wins the Dorothy Canfield Fisher Children's Book Award.

1981 *A Ring of Endless Light* is nominated for the John Newbery Medal; *A Swiftly Tilting Planet* earns the Newbery Honor Award.

1982 *A Ring of Endless Light* wins the California Young Reader Medal.

1983 *A Ring of Endless Light* wins the Colorado Children's Book Award.

1986 L'Engle wins the ALAN Award for Outstanding Contribution to Adolescent Literature from the National Council of Teachers of English (NCTE).

1990 She wins the Kerlan Award.

1997 L'Engle wins the World Fantasy Convention Lifetime Achievement Award.

1998 She wins with the Margaret A. Edwards Award for Lifetime Achievement.

1998 L'Engle wins the Sophia Award from the School of Spiritual Psychology.

1999 She wins the Wisdom House Award.

2004 L'Engle is presented with the National Humanities Medal.

BIBLIOGRAPHY

Abbe, Elfrieda, Kevin Keefe, Ronald Kovach, Jeff Reich, and Phillip Martin. "Writers Who Make a Difference." *Writer* vol. 116, no. 1 (January 2003): p. 21.

"About Smith," Smith College. Available online. URL: http://www.smith.edu.

"Author Spotlight: Madeleine L'Engle," Random House Web site. Available online. URL: http://www.randomhouse.com/author/results.pperl?authorid=16446.

Behrman, Christine. "Review of *Many Water*," *School Library Journal*, Amazon.com. Available online. URL: http://www.amazon.com.

"The Best of the Century." *Time* (December 31, 1999): p. 73.

"The Booklist Interview: Madeleine L'Engle," Biography Resource Center. Available online. URL: http://galenet.galegroup.com/servlet/BioRC?vrsn=149&OP=contains&locID=bergen_resource.

Branch, Craig. "New Age Infiltrates American Life," Watchman Fellowship Inc. Available online. URL: http://www.geocities.com/Athens/Acropolis/8838/whine.html.

Burlin, Katrin. "Review of *Certain Women*," Biography Resource Center. Available online. URL: http://galenet.galegroup.com/servlet/BioRC?vrsn=149&OP=contains&locID=bergen_resource.

Carter, Alice T. "'*Wrinkle in Time*' Brings Drama to Science Center." *Pittsburgh Tribune*, April 20, 2004. Available online. URL: http://www.pittsburghlive.com/x/pittsburghtrib/s_190189.html.

Chase, Carole F. "Words of wisdom from Madeleine L'Engle." *Writer* vol. 115, no. 6 (June 2002): p. 26.

Coulter, Emilie. "Review of *A Swiftly Tilting Planet*," Amazon.com. Available online. URL: http://www.amazon.com.

Estes, Sally. "The Booklist Interview: Madeleine L'Engle." *Booklist* vol. 94, no. 18 (May 15, 1998): pp. 16–20.

Flores, Angelique. "'Everwood' Star Gets into 'Wrinkle.'" *Video Store Magazine* vol. 26, no. 50 (December 5–11, 2004): p. 12.

Gallo, Donald R. *Speaking for Ourselves.* Illinois: National Council of Teachers of English, 1990.

Hatch, Robert, and William Hatch. *The Hero Project*. New York: McGraw Hill, 2006.

Henneberger, Melinda. "I Dare You: Madeleine L'Engle on God, 'The Da Vinci Code,' and Aging Well." *Newsweek Entertainment* (May 7, 2004).

"Home Page," Ashley Hall Web Site. Available online. URL: http://www.ashleyhall.org.

Horowitz, Shel. "Madeleine L'Engle; Faith During Adversity." Frugal Fun Web site. Available online. URL: http://www.frugalfun.com/l'engle.html.

Kelleher, Terry. "A Wrinkle in Time: ABC review." *People Weekly* vol. 61, no. 19 (May 17, 2004): p. 38.

Kim, Caroline. "Telling Stories." *Humanities* vol. 26, no. 1 (Jan/Feb 2005): p. 21.

L'Engle, Madeleine. *A Circle of Quiet*. New York: Farrar, Straus & Giroux, 1972.

———. "Is It Good Enough for Children?" *The Writer* vol. 113.7 (July 2000): p. 8.

———. *Madeleine L'Engle Herself: Reflections on a Writing Life*. Compiled by Carole F. Chase. Colorado: Waterbrook Press, 2001.

———. "Margaret A. Edwards Award Acceptance Speech," Madeleine L'Engle Web site. Available online. URL: http://www.madeleinelengle.com.

———. *The Summer of the Great-Grandmother*. New York: Farrar, Straus & Giroux, 1974.

———. *Two-Part Invention*. New York: Farrar, Straus & Giroux, 1988.

———. *A Wrinkle in Time*. New York: Farrar, Straus & Giroux, 1962.

Lombardo, Cindy. "Review of *A Swiftly Tilting Planet*," *School Library Journal*, Amazon.com. Available online. URL: http://www.amazon.com.

Macneille, Suzanne. "Coming of Age: Mostly a Matter of Time." *New York Times*, May 9, 2004, pp. 13–14.

"Madeleine (Camp Franklin) L'Engle." InfoTrac. Available online. URL: http://infotrac.galegroup.com/itw/infomark/319/733/94517856w6/purl=rcl_CA_0_H100.

"Madeleine L'Engle," Biography Resource Center. Available online. URL: http://galenet.galegroup.com/servlet/BioRC?vrsn=149&OP=contains&locID=bergen_resource.

"Margaret A. Edwards Award," American Library Association. Avail-able online. URL: http://www.ala.org/ala/yalsa/booklistsawards/margaretaedwards/margaretedwards.htm.

Rafeal, Nick. " 'Wrinkle' A Fantastic Journey." *Boston Globe*, May 9, 2004, p. 4.

"Review of *An Acceptable Time*," VOYA (Voice of Youth Advocates), Amazon.com. Available online. URL: http://www.amazon.com.

"Review of *The Other Dog*," *Publishers Weekly*, Amazon.com. Available online. URL: http://www.amazon.com.

"Review of *Troubling a Star*," *Publishers Weekly*, Amazon.com. Available online. URL: http://www.amazon.com.

"Review of *A Wind in the Door*," Amazon.com. Available Online. URL: . http://www.amazon.com.

Rogers, Susan L. "Review of *Troubling a Star*," *School Library Journal*, Amazon.com. Available online. URL: http://www.amazon.com.

Scaperland, Maria Ruiz. "Madeleine L'Engle: An Epic in Time," *St. Anthony Messenger*, June 2002, American Catholic Web site. Available online. URL: http://www.americancatholic.org/messenger/jun2000/feature1.asp.

Snelson, Karin. "A New Wrinkle: A conversation with Madeleine L'Engle." Amazon.com. Available online. URL: http://www.amazon.com/gp/feature.html?docId=6238.

Sonne, Lisa. "A Stardust Journey with A Wrinkle in Time." Introduction to *A Wrinkle in Time*, by Madeline L'Engle. New York: Farrar, Straus & Giroux, 1962. Reprinted on Barnes and Noble Web site. Available online. URL: http://search.barnesandnoble.com/Wrinkle-in-Time/Madeleine-LEngle/e/9780374386139.

Talcroft, Barbara L. "Review of *A Wrinkle in Time*," Children's Literature, Amazon.com. Available online. URL: http://search.barnesandnoble.com/Wrinkle-in-Time/Madeleine-LEngle/e/9780312367541/?itm=1.

Townsend, John Rowland. "A Sense of Story: Essays on contemporary Writers for Children," Biography Resource Center Web site. Available online. URL: http://galenet.galegroup.com.

Trescott, Jacqueline. "A Gold Medal Day for Artists and Scholars; White House Honors Ray Bradbury, Madeleine L'Engle and 14 Others." *Washington Post*, November 18, 2004, p. C.4.

"Spirituality Café." *U.S. Catholic* vol. 68, no. 12 (December 2003): p. 23.

"Who We Are," National Endowment for the Humanities. Available online. URL: http://www.neh.gov/whoweare/awards.html.

"World Fantasy Awards," SciFi.com. Available online. URL: http://scifipedia.scifi.com/index.php/World_Fantasy_Award.

"A 'Wrinkle' in Primetime." *School Library Journal* vol. 47, no. 7 (July 2001): p. 19.

Zarin, Cynthia. "The Storyteller; Profiles." *New Yorker* vol. 80, no. 8 (April 12, 2004): p. 60.

FURTHER READING

Gallo, Donald R. *Speaking for Ourselves.* Urbana, Ill.: National Council of Teachers of English, 1990.

Gonzalez, Doreen. *Madeleine L'Engle: Author of* A Wrinkle in Time. New York: Dillon Press, 1991.

Hatch, Robert, and William Hatch. *The Hero Project.* New York: McGraw-Hill, 2006.

Hein, Rolland, and Clyde S. Kilby. *Christian Mythmakers: C.S. Lewis, Madeleine L'Engle, J.R.R. Tolkien, George MacDonald, G.K. Chesterton and Others.* Chicago: Cornerstone Press, 2002.

L'Engle, Madeleine. *Madeleine L'Engle Herself.* Colorado Springs, Colo.: Waterbrook Press, 2001.

Rosenberg, Aaron. *Madeleine L'Engle.* New York: Rosen, 2006.

Yunghans, Penelope. *Prize Winners: Ten Writers for Young Readers.* Greensboro, N.C.: Morgan Reynolds, 1995.

Web Sites

Madeleine L'Engle's Official Web Site
http://www.madeleinelengle.com

The Wheaton College Archives and Special Collections: Madeleine L'Engle Papers
http://www.wheaton.edu/learnres/ARCSC/collects/sc03

PICTURE CREDITS

page:

10: Reprinted with permission of Crosswicks, Ltd. and McIntosh & Otis, Inc.

18: AP Images

21: © Atlantide Phototravel/ Corbis

26: © Bettmann/CORBIS

31: Reprinted with permission of Crosswicks, Ltd. and McIntosh & Otis, Inc.

38: Reprinted with permission of Crosswicks, Ltd. and McIntosh & Otis, Inc.

42: Library of Congress, 3b46036

50: Reprinted with permission of Crosswicks, Ltd. and McIntosh & Otis, Inc., copyright © Beverly Hall

56: © Bettmann/CORBIS

60: ABC/Photofest

68: Reprinted with permission of Crosswicks, Ltd. and McIntosh & Otis, Inc.

70: Reed Saxon, AP Images

74: Reprinted with permission of Crosswicks, Ltd. and McIntosh & Otis, Inc.

78: Reprinted with permission of Crosswicks, Ltd. and McIntosh & Otis, Inc.

88: Reprinted with permission of Crosswicks, Ltd. and McIntosh & Otis, Inc.

92: Reprinted with permission of Crosswicks, Ltd. and McIntosh & Otis, Inc.

INDEX

ABOUT THE CONTRIBUTOR

TRACEY BAPTISTE is a former elementary school teacher and textbook editor. She read *A Wrinkle in Time* when she was 12 and has loved L'Engle's work ever since. She now writes fiction and nonfiction books for children and young adults. You can read more about Ms. Baptiste at www.traceybaptiste.com.